( )

Amy Arnold lives in Cumbria. She has degrees in Music and Psychology, and studied postgraduate Neuropsychology at Birmingham University. She's worked as a university lecturer, teacher and swede packer. Her debut novel, *Slip of a Fish*, won the 2018 Northern Book Prize and was shortlisted for the 2019 Goldsmiths Prize.

Lori & Joe
Amy Arnold

For Jocelyn and Amber

Lori & Joe

To be in the fog is to be in a state of suspension. What's true is then not true: the mind's liberation.
    Etel Adnan, *Sea and Fog*

The kitchen,
somewhere in South Lakeland,
late November 1999

IT'S EARLY, IT ISN'T QUITE LIGHT, AND THE FOG IS DOWN OVER THE FELL

Still down, Lori thinks, and she rubs at her eye again, and well, she hasn't exactly given it much of a chance to clear, no, she shouldn't go expecting miracles with the eye when she's only just got herself out of bed, and Lori stands there at the kitchen window and looks out over the valley. The third day of fog, she thinks, or the fourth. She'd be hard pushed to remember fog settling like this, sitting over the fell, for days on end, and if anyone's going to remember anything about fog on the fell it's her, and well, it doesn't pay to go thinking about the number of hours she's spent looking out of this window. They add up, she thinks, if you do the same thing morning after morning for years on end it's bound to add up, and Lori looks out over the valley at the fog and she thinks, if anything it's creeping down. Moor Head to the quarry overnight, she thinks, and she turns and looks at the coffee sitting there on the side. She can leave the coffee for a while, yes, she's only just started on the coffee, and she puts her hand up to rub her eye. Grit, she thinks, whether Joseph can see it or not, yes, it's there when she blinks.

Imagine having to brace yourself every time, she said, and he had her stand out on the porch. He pulled her lower eyelid down with his thick fingers.

No grit in there, love.

And Lori looks out across the valley at the fell, and well, doesn't she always think that darkness uncovers the fell, or at least the shape of the fell, yes, the fog is the one that takes, the fog moves in without fear or favour, she thinks, and she'll let the coffee brew, she'll let it sit

5

and it's both eyes really, and Lori puts her hand over the
left eye, then the right eye, and she thinks, the right one's
almost as bad, and well, yes, she knew that, she knows that.
Forget the eyes, she thinks, the eyes will clear by lunchtime,
although she has to say that the whole business has made
her take a bit more care up there in the bedroom first thing,
yes, it's only a matter of time before the carpet catches
her out, all its little rucks and wrinkles. Landmines, she
thinks, and well, she should be done with things like that
at her age, she should be stepping down onto something
soft and fluffy now she can see the big six-o up ahead,
although she isn't there yet, no, she isn't all that far north
of fifty, and the coffee can sit. Leave it, she thinks, and
aren't they always saying take the carpet up, get rid of the
carpet once and for all, when they haven't so much as
pulled up a corner on the east-facing wall where the damp
comes in. And Lori looks out over the valley, and she
thinks, fog or mist? clag? and no, there won't be any point
in starting on the carpet until spring comes around. Let it
dry out, she thinks, because she's hardly mistaken when
she says there are a hundred things to do before getting
around to the carpet, and well, she can start with the
coffee, yes, pour the coffee out and take it up now. Too
much time at the window, she thinks, and she puts the
back of her hand up to rub the eye. Just the left one, she
thinks, leave it at that, and it still isn't quite light. The
light will be a while coming on, she thinks, if they're almost
in December, yes, another year gone in the blink of an eye,
and will she stop with the eyes? yes, that's enough talk
about eyes already, and Lori turns and sees the coffee there
on the side, and well, she knows she's gone and left it too
long again.

Joseph will bang through. Any minute now he'll reach for his stick, and she thinks, hold on, yes, wait for it, and she stands at the kitchen window looking up at the ceiling and she thinks, what are you doing now Lori Fitzgerald? get on up there with the coffee, go on up and say your piece.

At least it's been well-brewed, yes, that's what she says, she says more or less the same thing every morning. You have to say something, she thinks, and she puts the back of her hand up to her eye, and the stick's only a joke. She knows that, yes, she knows about the stick, but she can't help anticipating. And Lori stands in the kitchen and looks up at the ceiling. Hold on, she thinks, wait for it.

And she'll put the heating on before she goes up with the coffee, yes, they can afford to have the heating going for an hour on a November morning, and she looks up at the ceiling and she looks out over the valley at the fell and she thinks it's about time she paid the fell a visit, if winter's almost on them, if she's starting to think about having the heating on again, and Lori looks over at the laurel and she looks over at the fog there on the side of the fell and she thinks, not even a breeze. Good enough, she thinks, and she knows that she'll be waiting right past Christmas and into the New Year if she's waiting for a perfect day for walking, and even then, she thinks, yes, even then, and the last thing she wants to do today is hang around here at home whilst the boys talk bike. Although they're hardly boys, she thinks, you couldn't make up a full head of hair between them. And Lori turns and sees the bike leaning up against the kitchen table and she thinks, well, help yourself Joe, yes, go ahead, because everything's the bike with him these days, isn't it? it's been nothing but the bike since the day he retired and now the house is filling up with magazines, with components, it's almost getting too much, and well, a few magazines is one thing, Lori thinks, yes, you can stack a few magazines and put them in a corner somewhere, but two rear cassettes in the outside loo, no, no, she can't produce a thing in there with those cogs, those teeth, gleaming right at her, and she'd drop the whole matter if it ended there. She isn't so small-minded that she can't see her way past a few components and magazines, but there's the bike itself, the *Chambéry*, the *LeMond Chambéry*. Like a king, she thinks, yes, it's the kind of name you have to announce. Which seems unfair, she thinks, when the cat doesn't have a name, when the cat still trots around the place as nameless as the day she arrived, and Lori turns and looks at the bike leaning up against the kitchen table and she looks at the clock there on the wall and she thinks, still early, too early for banging through, although she can't help anticipating. He's drilled it into her, she thinks, and she pours out the coffee, yes, go ahead with the coffee now, and of course, Lori thinks, Joseph is expecting the boys tomorrow, yes, Saturday for the boys, not today, and she turns and looks back over at the fog and she thinks she'll go out for a walk anyway, she'll have a morning on the fells, and she thinks, what's *Chambéry* anyway? what is that? and well, whatever it is it'll have to go. The kitchen's small enough, yes, aren't they always saying, aren't we always? she thinks, and she promised herself last night that she'd deal with it this morning. You can't go bringing up important matters before bed, Lori thinks. Nobody wants to sleep on an open wound. And she's seen the way he touches it, she's seen him run his hand along the top tube when they're eating, yes, a fork in one hand, his other hand on the top tube. It's almost a caress, she thinks. It's almost loving. And he

8

can wheel it out to the shed after they've had coffee because it's nothing but talk with the boys anyway. Cadence
and power, drafting and slipstreams. The *Chambéry* itself
never moves, no, he's had it up against the table since summer and well, at least she hasn't had to wash his Lycras for
months. That's been more than a small blessing, she thinks,
and she'll go on up with the coffee now and later this morning she'll walk up onto the fell, and Lori looks over at the
laurel and she looks over at the fog on the fell and she feels
a flutter of excitement. It lifts her up and sets her down.
And she thinks, get your stick Joe, pick up your stick and
bang through then.

Coffee, she says. And she promised herself last night she'd
say something to Joe about the bike. Yes, get the *Chambéry*
out of the kitchen once and for all, she thinks, and she
goes on up a few steps and she thinks, not *Chambéry*, no,
not with the *r* sitting there in the front of the mouth.

Like this, love. As if you're about to gargle, she thinks,
and well, she's never been any good at gargling either.
That's another thing she can't do, she thinks, and when
it comes to doing anything like that, when it comes to any
sort of performance, she means, she hasn't got a cat in
hell's chance of getting it right and she thinks, forget it,
forget *Chambéry*, yes, she'll say *LeMond*, she can bluff
the *d* if she needs to, yes, easier to bluff the *d* than risk
Chambéry, and Lori walks on up the stairs.

Coffee, she says, and she'll give the eye a good rub
when she's put the coffee down. Hold on with the eye for
now, she thinks, and after they've had coffee she'll go
walking up on the fell, and it must be the third morning
they've woken to fog, if not the fourth, she thinks, yes,
she'd struggle to remember another time like it, and Lori
walks on up the stairs with the coffee and she imagines
herself walking down the bridleway to the church, she
imagines herself crossing the little bridge over the beck,
and here she is again, here she is on the stairs with two
mugs of coffee. One for Joseph and one for her, and she
pushes open the bedroom door with her foot.

Coffee, she says, and she thinks, put the coffee down
then rub the eyes. Both of them, because there isn't any use
in pretending it's only the left, and it's still so early. It still

isn't quite light and Lori stands inside the bedroom door and looks across the room and out into the valley and well, look at that, she thinks, the tups are out with the ewes at last, and she'll put the coffee down and rub her eyes, God, yes, that's one thing that really can't wait, she thinks, and Lori says, coffee, and she looks over at the bed and she thinks, something isn't right over there, no, something isn't quite as it usually is, and she stands inside the bedroom door with the two mugs of coffee and she thinks, look again, yes, look more carefully, and she takes a little step towards the bed.

Joseph's dead, she thinks. And she thinks, what are you doing Joe? what are you doing with your face all contorted like that? and she thinks, no, wait, it isn't the face, why does she think it's the face when really the face is almost normal? yes, if the face is anything it's only pale, although she's seen it paler and she thinks, eyes then, always the eyes, yes, she would have guessed on the eyes without looking even, and she thinks, put the coffee down, God, yes, unburden yourself of the coffee at least, and Lori puts one of the mugs down on her bedside table. She walks around the bed and she puts the other mug down and she thinks, let it go there, where it always goes, and she takes a couple of steps over towards the window.

The carpet, she thinks, the bloody carpet's a liability, and she rubs her eyes and she sees that, yes, the tups are out on the in-bye with the ewes at last. Lambing will come late then, she thinks. No lambs until the end of April at least, yes, they'll be waiting a while for lambs, she thinks, and she knows it's stupid, standing there at the bedroom window looking out across the valley thinking about what to say next, and she knows that whatever

she says will be as if it was never said, but still she turns
to the bed.

Joe, she says, the fog has settled on the fell.

Lori pulls the garden gate behind her until she hears the latch. It really must be early still, she thinks, and she looks down the lane. She looks right, then left, and there isn't anyone. Get going then, she thinks, and she starts on down the bridleway, one foot in front of the other, and she thinks, simple, yes, with feet it's almost always simple, and Lori walks on down and she looks across the valley and up at the fog on the fell, then she looks into the white sky and she thinks, a good morning for the time of year, a fine morning even, what with the tups out on the in-bye with the ewes at last, and she walks on down the bridleway into the valley and she hears the water running between the stones at her feet and she thinks, it's so early, nothing's begun, and she pulls up the zip on her jacket although it isn't exactly cold, no, she can see by the colour of the place that they haven't broken in to winter yet, and Lori thinks of all the rain they've been having these last months. After a while it runs right through, she thinks, and she looks over at the fell, at the bracken and stone and grass, and she looks at the thick moss on the stone walls either side of her and she thinks, something has to thrive. Let it, she thinks, because things will come right by spring. And Lori rubs at the eye although the eye's almost cleared and it's really only the right one that causes her trouble, and hardly any, Lori thinks, and she makes her way down into the valley. It's a good morning, she thinks. We aren't anywhere close to freezing yet, and she looks up at the heavy sky and well, no, she wouldn't say heavy, but the sky has come down to meet the fell, and Lori looks from east to west because there's almost always a fracture to be found.

And well, no, not today. White, from end to end. This is how it'll be then, Lori thinks, this is how it'll turn out, and thank God, because she wasn't going to go putting the bucket out in the back room before she left the house. She's sick of being the one who does the bucket, or at least remembers the bucket. Joseph has to be asked, she thinks, and if they just got the back roof sorted then there wouldn't be all this friction between them every time it rains. Yes, get the back roof done, Lori thinks, all it needs is a sheet of polycarbonate, that's what she's been told, it's an afternoon's work, a day at the most, yes, she could ignore the problem with the main roof if they got someone in to do the back one. Joseph knows people, she thinks. She's been saying the same things for years, she sends herself round and round in circles and the rain will hold off today, for a few hours at least. She won't be out long. Up the fell and back down, that's all she'll do today, and if a few drops of rain get in it's hardly a big deal, no, the bucket only needs to be out when the rain's really hammering and well, she can see it isn't going to end up like that today, no, it's far from a bad day for the time of year, Lori thinks.

And that's four dead bodies she's seen now. The number goes on rising, and well, it will, she thinks, there's only one direction of travel where that's concerned, and everything was the same this morning. She looked across the room and out into the valley.

Coffee, she said. She always says the same thing. Twice on the stairs she says it, twice in the bedroom and of course it's coffee, it's always coffee, and she has to admit she's been expecting this, yes, it was anything but a surprise to see Joe laid out on the bed with his eyes pinned to the ceiling, and she thinks, not the ceiling, no, his eyes pinned to the woodchip wallpaper, which is sad, she thinks, and the woodchip is hardly her fault, no, she warned him enough times. Don't start with the woodchip, Joe.

It'll cover all the imperfections, love, it'll –

And they call each other love, although it doesn't always get through, no, the longer you know each other the harder it is to penetrate, and well, you start in one place and finish in another. *My Lo, my love,* yes, it's easy to see how things mutate, and Joe, my Joe, laid out on the bed first thing, she thinks. She's been expecting it, rehearsing it even, yes, every morning she pushes the bedroom door with her breath half held. She treads cautiously, which is nothing to do with the carpet because the carpet's just fine over there by the door.

Coffee, she says. She almost sings it, and she thinks, not sings, Joe's the one who sings. There isn't room for another singer about the place.

Coffee. Coffee, she says, and the valley and the fell just sit there. They haven't moved as much as an inch in all this time, in twenty-five years, Lori thinks, and it's always the eyes. It's unnatural to fixate. Although how can she go around saying that when she's only seen four dead bodies, and out of those only two pairs of eyes? or does she mean sets of eyes? no, pairs, she thinks, and she isn't going to go including the old woman at the bus station in this, no, forget about her, Lori thinks, and eyes or no eyes it was her mother who went first, which was probably the right order of things, yes, nothing wrong in that, Lori thinks, and on the evening of the day her father died she'd said to Joe, do you know where he's gone? she was looking out of the kitchen window, the sun had just about left the valley, and well, she can't blame him for pouring himself another glass of wine and holding the bottle out.

Drink, love?

She'd shaken her head. She'd had him pinned, she'll admit that now. Do you know where he's gone? do you know where they go? That's what she'd said, and she'd thought, stammer your way out of that one, and she'd looked out of the window and left him to tie himself up with his Ds and his Ns and when he'd finally finished she turned around and held her hand out for the bottle. Always Ds and Ns, she thinks, but it hardly happens these days, does it, nobody would ever know, and leaving him with the woodchip was the right thing to do. The last thing she wants is to get mixed up in anything complicated. God, yes, she hasn't got the stamina for messing, for meddling, she thinks, and all things considered four isn't too many, four is probably the average number of bodies you see in a lifetime, and she won't include the old woman at the bus station because every time she thinks back to that day she can't be sure she saw her dead, no, it wouldn't be strictly true to say she's seen five. Four, yes, four dead bodies, plus the woman at the bus station.

And she's already crossed the beck. If she turns and looks back, she'll see their little house and the pike rising steeply up behind it, although she won't look, no, she'll head on up this bit of bridleway, cross the Garburn and go on up to the intake wall, she thinks, and hasn't she always had a good pair of legs to carry her?

The legs will be the last to go, she's sure enough of that and if there's anything that's weak, it's the stomach. The stomach's always causing trouble one way or the other and she'll just get on up this bit of bridleway and cross the

Garburn, or is it Dubbs? she thinks, because she doesn't strictly know where Dubbs Road becomes Garburn Road, becomes Garburn Pass, Crabtree Brow, although more or less, yes, she more or less knows, and well, it takes a good, long time to absorb these things. It takes a hundred encounters, a thousand, Lori thinks, to pass blindly from unknowing to knowing, the way a child does, and well, yes, she's sure that's the way children do it because every time they had a new baby next door she thought it would never learn to stand on its own two feet, never say an older brother's name. By the time a *Felix*, an *Emile*, cut through the babble it was as if it had always been there, perfectly formed, Lori thinks. And Thwaites and Howes and Folds come as easily as Streets and Crescents these days, more easily even. They've worked their way inside her like a slow-acting poison. Although, once an offcomer, Lori thinks. And they've lived here twenty-five years, they came up on a whim, and the first time they crossed their little yard Joe held her hand. They'd only been together one winter. One winter, and the whole of it spent in his room or her room, or down in his music room, and they crossed their little yard hand in hand. It was the first time she'd seen him in broad daylight. She'd thought his hair was black! And well, no, not black, not quite dark brown, which hardly matters now, and neither does the fact that he packed up his father's car and drove the pair of them up the M6 with nothing but the vaguest idea of what they'd do when they arrived. That's how it was, Lori thinks, although she doesn't remember why, no, she doesn't really, because it wasn't as if there was anything much wrong with the way things were back home. We were happy. More or less, Lori thinks, and she pictures herself getting on the little train to Joe's. She pictures her jeans, her jacket, that blue canvas bag she had. Through Cradley Heath, Lori thinks, through Old Hill, Rowley Regis, and she pictures the streets bending and folding. Like intestines, Lori thinks, and then, yes, the anticipation of seeing him. It was a mild winter, the kindest she can remember, and they'd liked the life well enough. He'd had his music room, his mother's Bechstein, and Lori thinks, why did we, if we were happy enough? and no, she doesn't really, she's never really.

And Lori pictures the pair of them walking up the bridle-way to their little house, and she sees that the rain is coming down as usual and that even though the bridleway is narrow, too narrow to walk side by side, they're holding hands, yes, she sees herself hanging back a bit, half a step.
    And isn't it always raining, Joe says, isn't it always chucking it down around here? he honestly can't believe how much rain comes out of the sky above their little house. They certainly wouldn't call this spring down south, no, it hardly qualifies as an April shower, he says. And as far as he can remember he's never had more than a quick drenching in spring, a quick spit, as he likes to say, although he supposes that can't be right, no, he's sure it must rain like this back home but he can't for the life of him picture it raining, and Lori says yes, the rain they get here is like no other rain, none she can remember, and Joe squeezes her hand and he says, my Lo, my love, and she says in any case they definitely notice the rain more, now they have to walk the mile to the bus stop, probably closer to two miles in fact, and if you're carrying things all the way back up the hill, if you've got a bag of shopping or something, she says, and Joe says, yes, but you give up one thing and in its place,

and he kisses her on the cheek and she feels that both the lips and the cheek need to be wet to get a feeling like that, and Lori says, kiss me again and he kisses her on the forehead, long and slow, and afterwards he takes a step back and he says, there are worse things than rain. Far worse. And Lori looks up the bridleway, she looks at their little house. Come on then, she says, and she takes his hand.

Lori and Joe, Joe and Lori. That's how we are, she says.

Who, Lo. *Who* we are, he says, and if there's one thing he misses, yes, he'll say this now. Above all else, he says, and Lori lets go of his hand and she says, wait, wait, if there's one thing she misses it's the dog, it's Big Ranulph, because there's been a dog at home ever since she was small, and for a while they had two dogs, but now there's only Big Ranulph and she misses him so much that sometimes she thinks she hears his paws scattering across the flagstones. Even though it's the wrong house, she says, the wrong house for the dog, and they go on walking up the bridleway towards their little house and Joe says he doesn't know about dogs, that a dog is the kind of thing you've got to be sure about, a dog is a commitment and a half. No, he just can't get his head around her missing Big Ranulph the way she does and Lori thinks, the rain, this rain, it keeps on coming, and he says the thing he misses, if she didn't already know. The piano. Of course. And he says his mother played to him before he was born, Chopin and Liszt, all the Romantics. He was destined to be a musician, yes, that was surely his destiny, he says, because when it comes to the piano his mother's got the finest touch. She plays as if she's playing a violin, a cello, as if she's singing, he says, and you have to appreciate, Lo, that a piano is really a percussion instrument, that essentially you're hitting at something, and Lori says yes, she understands that, and she supposes Joe must be a good musician if he went to the School of Music, although she can never remember which School of Music he went to. *The* School of Music, yes, *The* School of Music, she thinks, and Joe says, without the piano it feels as though something's been severed, and he knows severed is a strong word, but nonetheless, he says, and he isn't saying he doesn't like to sing, singing is the thing that holds him, but a piano is to a musician as a stethoscope is to a doctor, if she understands where he's coming from, and Lori says yes, she understands, and she nods her head and she thinks, the rain, it's relentless. And he'll get the Bechstein brought up. He can't think of anything he'd rather do right now than get his fingers around the rest of the Prokofiev.

Are you familiar with it, Lo? Sonata number seven? And he'll sing the opening. Yes, wait, he says, and Lori thinks, listen to him, placing every note with, and she thinks, with. With affection, and Lori rubs her eye with the back of her hand and she thinks, is the right one the bad one? Because she's always saying one eye's worse than the other eye and she never can remember.

It was Finzi he had us listen to later, Lori thinks, and she rubs her eye, and she rubs her other eye and she sees the pair of them standing in the living room, Joe and Lori, Lori and Joe, and she hears the music coming out from the speakers. Piano music, she thinks, and she listens to the piano and she hears a weight inside its notes, a familiar weight, and she thinks, of course the piano is a percussion instrument, yes, sometimes the notes need to be struck, yes, she hears it almost as easily as she hears the rain at the

window, and she listens to the piano, she hears it drop its
heavy notes, one note after the other it drops and well,
she hardly would have recognised it before but, yes, the
rain up here has this same weight, and she hears the notes
coming out into the living room and it's as if she knows
that rain will be made over and over again, and she thinks,
for all eternity, if she can let herself think like that, and she
looks over at Joe and he opens his mouth and out comes a
sound that hardly belongs to him, no, the sound belongs
there with the piano, she thinks, and she closes her eyes
and the piano makes its heavy notes and she hears Joe sing
and she turns and looks out of the window, and she sees
that the fell has almost disappeared inside the music, and
well, let the music take the fell, she thinks, because all
things considered the fell's a lot to handle from a window
when she's used to front doors and living room windows,
to streets bending and folding around her like intestines,
and now, yes, she feels so far from home, and she thinks
it's probably the music that's making her feel like this,
yes, almost all music makes her feel so far from home or
as if she's never been home, and she hears Joe sing and she
thinks, we don't belong here. Joseph, my Joe, and if the
weight comes from anywhere it's from behind the notes,
because there isn't anything in the notes themselves, and
she hears Joe sing, she hears the words *and earth*, she hears
the words *and air*, *and rain* and she hears that *rain* is neither
finished nor unfinished. And now she'll cry, she thinks,
because she almost understands what those words mean,
yes, all the weather they have now, all this rain, she thinks,
it strips something away from you, and Lori wraps her
arms around herself and looks out across the valley at the
fell and she thinks, it'll come down all night.

And Lori rubs at both eyes, at the left eye, then the right eye, and she thinks, yes, we had music all the time, we had singing. And she thinks, it doesn't pay to rhapsodise, because if she's sure of one thing it's that she didn't always like the music that poured out into their living room, no, sometimes the music would speak and sometimes it wouldn't and she doesn't know the first thing, she doesn't even know what an aria is, and she thinks, how can you marry a musician and not know about arias, or lieder? how can a relationship like that ever?

And she thinks, no. He can go out to the yard. If he really has to sing he can take himself out there, and why does he still need to? she thinks, no, she's never understood why he still needs to, and as far as she's concerned he's altogether better outside than in, she thinks, because if there's one thing that gets to her it's the shuffling, it's those fucking slippers, and already she's thinking it again, thinking, pick up your feet Joe, and he won't sit through more than the news headlines these days. He'll keep his hand pressed flat on the arm of the sofa, readying himself, Lori thinks, and it isn't going too far to say she feels the tension her end, yes, it comes across the back strut and in through her head, and she'll have to give up on leaning back the way she likes to because she can't be thinking about the tension in Joseph's arm if she wants to keep abreast of what's happening in the world, and well, she'd be hard pushed to say what actually is happening. She can't think, no, well, no, she can't, and last night was a bad one.

That's enough for me, love, he said, and she feels it her end of the sofa, yes, it takes him forever to push himself up and out and almost every evening she sits there watching the news headlines with her teeth all tight thinking, pillock. She thinks it again when he pushes himself across the flagstones in those slippers.

Nobody thinks pillock, Lori thinks. And the slippers have got open backs. He curls his toes when he walks. He must do, she thinks, and well, she wastes far too much time conjuring up images of his toes inside his socks, inside his slippers, yes, she's only got to hear him scraping and she starts conjuring. He'll end up with hammer toe, she thinks, or does she mean claw toe, and she thinks, last night was a bad one, yes, slippers as usual, then all that trouble trying to get the lid off the honey jar and she likes to watch the news, yes, they'll sit themselves down a few minutes before nine.

The *Nine O'Clock News*, Lori says, and she thinks, Peter Sissons is going strong at least, yes, Peter Sissons can't be more than a few years off Joe, one side or the other, although it's hardly fair to compare, she thinks, if Peter Sissons went to Oxford University, which must be a notch above Joe's School of Music, and she thinks, you're a pillock yourself. Four O levels. Almost five, she thinks, and she'd be hard pushed to remember last night's head-lines. An earthquake in Greece? Somewhere over there, she thinks, and well, it goes to show she isn't totally oblivious, yes, it's good to know some of it gets through despite his shuffling, and she'd heard him in the kitchen with the honey jar, she'd heard his little squeezing sounds, she'd almost shouted out.

The house can't cope with the noise, she thinks. She's only got to spill a few grains of rice or sugar over the flagstones and the whole kitchen throbs, and she's spent enough time teaching herself to be careful with that over the years, yes, she's earned herself a steady hand and she thinks, Joe isn't bothered. It's as and when with him, yes, all his little voyages across the flagstones. Every time she hears him she thinks, pick your feet up, Joe, or just wear socks. Yes, wear socks! And why's she saying that now? Doesn't she understand? No, well, no, she thinks, because she can't get herself over the shuffling, the sound of felt against stone, she means, and she lines up her incisors, she holds them for a slow ten or until she feels her jaw twitch. The left side gives up first, she thinks, yes, she's weaker on the left, it's the same with the eye, or is it the right side with the eye? And Lori walks on up the bridleway and she thinks, we're done with the shuffling then. Yes, she got what she asked for in the end, and she walked right in on him with that honey jar last night. She stood in the doorway and watched him wrestle with the lid, and what is it his hand makes her think of when it grips like that, when it clamps down? A creature of some sort, a tarantula, a mantis maybe, Lori thinks, and this is the fourth time, yes, his is the fourth body she's set eyes on.

Up and up, Lori thinks, which is the natural law of things. Until you go and intercept the line yourself, and she thinks, up this bit of bridleway to the intake wall. That's where it starts in earnest, yes, she never really feels as though she's walking until she's got herself over the stile and out onto the open fell and she did a double take with Joe this morning. She was standing inside the bedroom door with the coffee the way she always does, yes, always the same with her and the coffee, she thinks, and there must have been something nudging her to take another step towards the bed, and well, it won't have been one thing, no, she can't go around saying it was his eyes or his face or his arms. You can't boil everything down, she thinks, and he can get his hand around his stick in the half-light, yes, he gets to it without sitting up, without so much as a turn of the head, no, he doesn't do anything more than flop his arm out of the bed, grasp and tap, tap.

Hardly a tap, Lori thinks, he has a ruddy good bang with the thing, yes, he flops his left arm out, eyes shut, and no, she's made that bit up, she's inventing the eyes, *les yeux*, she thinks, and she still doesn't understand how *les yeux* grows out of *l'œil*. Everything he teaches her gets away. Glass eels, she thinks, little elvers, and if anything ruins a person it's an education. If anything brings you to a grinding halt, and she thinks, Latin and French, three long years at the School of Music and he's always gone for a heavy pudding, a jam roly-poly. Even his slippers are heavy, yes, somehow his slippers weigh, she thinks, and her eyes were bad this morning. Both eyes. She stood inside the bedroom door with the coffee thinking, put the coffee down then rub at the eyes. Coffee, she said, and of course she said coffee, she says the same thing every day. Coffee, yes, here's your coffee love, and she looked out across the valley. Yes, watch the light come on, give yourself an anchor, she thinks, a solid handle on the day, and it can't have been more than a few hours ago. Already she's struggling to think how it was. Yes, in with the coffee, she thinks, up the stairs and in with the coffee, and Lori pictures herself standing a step or two inside the bedroom door and she pictures herself looking over at Joe lying there in the bed, and well, she can't really remember, can't really see, and if she doesn't make an effort to get it back now that'll be it, because she's never heard of anything that came back once it had gone, well, no, she thinks, and she'd thought Fergus was a doll that day. She'd thought she heard his eyes click-clack, *les yeux*, *l'œil*, and how on earth do you go about pronouncing *œ*, she thinks. Not *oh*, *ee*. No, not that, and she thinks, shut up, will you? because even if she gets the *œ* she'll never get the *i* next to the *l*, and she thinks, give up with French, we never go further south than Morecambe anyway. No, she doesn't even want to go as far as London, let alone Paris, the Dordogne or wherever it is people like to go and she thinks, he never looked as though he was staying anyway, however heavy his slippers might be. And when the music stops it's gone, she thinks, the music's only ever on its way out, and she thinks, catch him now, if you can, and she holds him there on the bed, she holds is stiff face, his stiff eyes and she thinks, if it's anything at all it's the eyes, yes, the body never seems to catch up.

Just her hands. It isn't anything more than the hands and perhaps here around her middle, although she thinks, not really, no, it hasn't come in around her middle yet, and she thinks, give the hands a quick shake, a quick clap, and it won't be anything more than up and down the fell for her today, no, it's hardly a day for hanging around, and Lori looks up at the white sky and she thinks, two kinds of white, one Machiavellian, and she stands there on the bridleway and pulls her jacket up to check she's all tucked in, T-shirt, shirt, and she feels the two scones she put in her jacket pocket before she came out, she feels them bulging and she thinks, of course, yes, Joseph must have wanted the honey for a scone last night. All that trouble with the lid, all his little squeezing sounds, and she knows for a fact that he's got to the end of the jam, God, yes, he's been going at the last of the jam for days. She'll have to get more in, although she doesn't touch it herself, no, a bit of butter's enough for her and out of the two of them he's the snacker. He could polish off a steak dinner and he'd still be up and snacking once the headlines are done. *Steak au poivre*, Lori thinks. If she even knew what steak *au poivre* is and every evening she sits there on the sofa lining up her incisors and think-ing he'll get claw toe, yes, if he goes on shuffling in those huge slippers he'll get something or other, and she thinks, they're size eleven and a half when he's lucky to be pushing a ten, although his hands are big, yes, his fingers are thick, sausage fingers, no use when it comes to packets and jars. Overkill, Lori thinks, and once in a while she finds herself saying, give it here, pass it here Joe. A packet of wagon wheels, a tin of John West. He hands them over like a child.

What happened? Lori thinks, because didn't he have
a few preludes and fugues under those fingers of his? didn't
he spend years and years with Bach? and in all likelihood
they could've squeezed the Bechstein in somewhere, yes,
a piano would have been a better bet than the TV. In the
long run, she thinks, and she couldn't care less about jars
and packets, about the way his face and fingers have set.
It happens to all men, she thinks, the features thicken, the
hair thins, and the cold has come in, although not all the
way, no, she's warm where it matters at least and she looks
up at the white sky and she thinks, the faintest wash of
paint, and anyone else would have phoned for a doctor or
an ambulance this morning, that's what anybody reasonable
would have done. But she hates the phone. She hates its
little semi-circular table, and Lori thinks of the table
standing there in the living room, she pictures it pushed
up against the wall.

Nobody phones anybody before the sun gets up, she
thinks. It scares people. And she carried his coffee back
downstairs, she poured it down the sink when she could've
had it herself, yes, she almost always makes herself a
second mug in the end anyway, and Lori looks down and
she sees herself striding over the loose stones and it's
true, every morning she finds herself at the window waiting
for her eyes to come back, for the coffee to brew, for Joseph
to bang through, yes, come bloody on, bang through, she
thinks, and if she doesn't wear socks the vibrations come
up through her tibia, almost to her knees. She tells herself
the house won't cope, but the house has been standing
almost three hundred years, and she had the coffee mugs.
Everything was the same. And Lori looks up at the white
sky and down into the gaping mouth of the valley. Coffee,

she says. Coffee. And she'll never hold a tune with a voice as small as that, although why's she even thinking about singing now? she doesn't have to sing another note ever again if she doesn't want to. She doesn't. Especially since Joe sings Bach out there in the yard, yes, it's Bach again, she thinks, everything's Bach again.

Radio 3's Composer of the Week, love.

And she thinks, pillock, she thinks, you absolute, and she'll not have him bringing Bach inside. The house won't cope, the house is on its last. And Lori looks along the valley and she sees the Tongue thrusting forward from the dale head. *Hier hast du die Seele*, she says. She does better with German, yes, once she'd got her head around the *w* and the *z* there wasn't anything for Joe to say apart from, ignore the umlauts for now, love, and well, we haven't gone back to umlauts, Lori thinks. She never liked the look of them anyway, all cramped up on his record covers, *Suiten für*, *Prelude für*.

Nobody says it in German, love.

We call each other love. It's a way of reminding ourselves, Lori thinks, and it probably isn't Bach anyway, *Hier hast du die Seele*, because she doesn't know the first thing about him, Bach, she means, or Schubert or any of those other Germans and she thinks, what kind of person can even tell one composer from the other anyway, and well, Joe would be a lot more useful if he had the first idea about how to fix the roof. Even the gutter would be a start. How many years? she thinks, listening to the water coming out of the break in the gutter. We haven't even got a ladder, no, he couldn't get up there to fix it if he wanted to, and she thinks, we've never been quite right, no, we've always been a bit off to one side and she thinks of the boys, the men over at the farm. They spend their whole lives making things work, Lori thinks, they're always tying up a gate or patching up a wall over there and well, she blames herself. She had no right to an educated man, she thinks, a man who went to the School of Music, and Lori stands there under the broad brush of sky and she knows for a fact there's more than one Bach, that J. S. Bach isn't the only Bach, and she says, *Hier hast du die Seele*. No umlauts there, no, we'll have to come back to umlauts, she thinks, and she can't be shaking, not that now too, and she looks down and she sees herself striding over the loose stones and she thinks, if it's really going to get cold, yes, if it's really going to go on like this all day then Joe'd be better off with the heating on. And she thinks, no, no heating, not if he's on the bed. The last thing she wants is a smell up there. It's something about the stone walls, she thinks, they hold on to it, but no, he won't smell, he only died this morning, last night maybe and she thinks, you can let a steak sit for a few hours. Although she knows nothing about steak, *steak au poivre*, get the *r* to the back of the throat love, and who was she supposed to call at that hour in the morning? who really? she thinks, and Lori looks along the length of the valley and she looks at the Tongue there and she thinks, there wasn't enough light to make him out clearly, bad eyes or no bad eyes, and well, she can't go throwing lights on first thing in the morning. Too jolting, she thinks, and he'll just have to get used to being left alone. He'll just have to manage in there. And what's she saying? it's worse than anthropomorphising, it's worse than the way she talks about the cat, the way she always asks Joseph if he thinks the cat looks relieved or bored. And he'll be glad of the company at least. If the cat's home, she means, and she looks at the sky and she thinks, if the sky's coming down on us. Although she knows about fog, yes, of all people, she thinks, and the cat will be home, the cat will be asleep on her chair, and at least she didn't bring in a mouse this morning, yes, most mornings Lori finds herself tossing a mouse or a head of a mouse out into the laurel. She doesn't look, no, she just picks it up and throws. And Joseph made it clear from the beginning that he wasn't going to go cleaning up corpses of any kind, mice, voles, birds, rats, she's your cat love, and he's kept to his word all right because he's never picked up so much as a feather. He doesn't see them. Yes, she's watched him step through fresh blood in those slippers more than a few times. You can't get blood out of felt once it's in. If she's told him once, she's told him, and she nags, God, yes, she really goes on and you'd think the cat would look repentant, guilty at least, although she knows for a fact that Joseph would never think like that, that he never has to stop himself from saying, don't you think she looks? which is the kind of thing Lori's always saying, or at least is almost always thinking, and this morning started well enough. If you start the day without a head it's a good day, and Lori thinks, always heads, although Annie from next door used to say it was gallbladders they were dodging, like little green pearls. And Lori looks at the low sky and she thinks, well what was Annie's cat called? and she thinks, Mikey or Monty or something. And it's going back a bit, too many years, and she thinks, Marshall maybe? although, no, it isn't going to come if she forces it, and she thinks, stop forcing and she looks down and she sees that she's really striding out, yes, look at that, she thinks, and when it comes to the Taylors she's made it a rule of sorts not to think about them, or at least not to dwell, and well, here she is now, walking up the bridleway trying to remember the name of their cat. The old cat, it could hardly bring its legs along with it when it walked, she thinks, and Lori pictures the cat sitting under the laurel and she thinks, it sat there to get out of the rain and when the sun came out it sat on the gas meter box and she thinks, not Marshall, no, and it's been too many years since the Taylors left, since she watched them pile in the back of their minibus, Emile first, she thinks, yes, Emile, then Felix. Silas was last.

And Lori looks up at the white sky. She won't be out long today, no, up and down the fell will be enough for her and there were so many children she hardly took any notice of the cat, although Joseph was always saying he couldn't imagine why they'd want a cat to add to their trouble.

Six children, those bloody chickens too.

And Lori thinks, Felix, Emile, Ross, Charlotte, Louise, Silas, and she looks up at the sky. She looks west, and if it's going to rain it won't be for hours yet and she says, Felix, Emile, Ross, Charlotte, Louise, Silas, and she half waits for the sound of Annie's voice. She half waits to hear that Annie's expecting again, that, surprise, there's another little one on the way and Lori feels herself breathing, she feels her chest pushing out and sucking in and she thinks, relax, you've got to, because she really can't go there today, to Annie and her endless string of babies. It's too much. All the congratulations she had to give, yes, congratulations, congratulations, too many congratulations and she thinks, it was never long before Annie was showing. She got to showing earlier and earlier, each baby a little bit earlier, Lori thinks, and she carried it all out front, yes, all that weight out there where you couldn't ignore it and Lori turns and looks back down the bridleway.

It's bleak, she thinks, or just cloudy, and she could probably still conjure up the shape of Annie's swollen belly if she wanted to. If you want to, she thinks, and it isn't as strange as all that, because didn't we live next door to each other for years? Our fertile years, Lori thinks, and she stops there on the path and shuts her eyes.

Too much trouble for one day, she thinks, and a low sky too, and of course she knows the shape of Annie's pregnant belly, it's almost as if it were her own belly, yes, that's how it is with the pair of them, Annie and Lori, Lori and Annie, and if she wants to she can conjure it up, and there, yes, there it is now, a sort of pressure, something pushing from the inside of her belly and Lori thinks, little hands, little feet, although she knows there can't be, no, she isn't so far gone that she doesn't know what is and isn't possible. Even so, Lori thinks, wouldn't it be ok to hitch her jacket up a little way now, slide her hands in under her T-shirt? and she thinks, no, not yet. And she had the coffee. The light was coming on so slowly. November light, Lori thinks, and she stands there on the path and she feels her chest push and stick and she feels the night still, pulling the day back into itself and she thinks, go on now, go on regardless, and she slides her hands in under her T-shirt and down into the warm and she thinks, right here, here, and she feels her belly, bulging out from her pubis and she thinks, little one, my tiny little and she feels her chest stutter, come loose, and she thinks, no matter the years. No, nothing ever changes and she thinks, one baby followed another. That's how things were with Annie. The babies kept coming. And she carries it all out front where everyone can see it, yes, she likes to make a show of it, and Lori thinks, let her, and she runs her hands up and over her belly and she thinks, be ever so gentle, because if there's room for a miracle in this world then here she is, if there's room for a bit of kindness. And Lori stands on the bridleway and she sees the huge flank of the fell coming out from under the fog. Its greens and browns and blacks, and she'd take herself off to the bedroom and lower herself onto the bed. All those years ago, she means, yes, she'd lower herself onto the bed and nine times out of ten they'd be out there in the yard or in the lane, Felix and Emile, then Ross, then Charlotte, Louise, Silas, although it was almost never all of them at once, she thinks, no, you hardly ever got all six together.

Eyes shut. That's what she told herself, keep your eyes shut, and she'd listen for Joseph, although she knew she was alone, that he always came home hours after she did, and she'd slip her hands in and feel for her swollen belly, yes, the same every time, Lori thinks, and she stands there on the bridleway and she runs her hands up and over and she thinks, gently now, ever so, and there was comfort in that, lying on the bed with nothing but her hands for company, and she never had to wait for long to feel something pressing, from the inside out. A small thing, but something nonetheless, Lori thinks, and there's been so much trouble today. It started so early. And now the cold's come in, yes, here's the cold after all, and Lori pulls her jacket down, she tugs it over her hips, and she feels the two scones bulging. Two scones, why did she take two when she wasn't hungry? She hasn't felt hungry all morning and if she'd known she was going to forget the cat's name she could have asked Joseph on his way up to bed last night. He would've stopped right there if she'd just said his name. He would have helped her think, because no, he wouldn't have wanted a thing like that hanging over them before bed

and a cat's name hardly matters, Lori thinks, and she'll
give up with thinking about the cat now. And the moment
she does she says, Marsalis. Marsalis! It takes her by surprise, the cat's name coming out of nowhere like that. She'd
almost convinced herself it was Marshall after all, and well,
here it is, Marsalis, Marsalis, and Lori hears something
at the edge of her voice, a little shake and she thinks, not
that now too, and she looks up at the white sky and well,
she knows how to walk off a bit of cold. She's done it more
times than she can remember, and she thinks, up the fell
and straight back down for you then. And this fell of theirs,
it's really only a baby fell, hardly the kind of fell to catch
people out the way some of them do. Scafell Pike, Lori
thinks, Blencathra, Helvellyn. No, there isn't anything
more sinister on top here than a mound of tough grass,
and once in summer, not many summers ago, perhaps only
two or three, she lay down when she got to the top. Under
a blue sky, Lori thinks. And she thinks, keep walking now,
keep on walking because it's impossible to get caught
out somewhere as familiar as this and when she looks out
across the valley each morning she likes to notice the way
the fell rises. Gracefully, she thinks, yes, that's what she
really thinks, that the fell sweeps upwards like a wave, that
there's motion in it, a sort of quickening, and Lori looks
down at her feet and she thinks, push on now, and it won't
be long before she crosses the Garburn and heads up onto
the fell itself and she thinks, the fog's been down for days,
three days, four, and this morning she woke to find it down
as low as the quarry here. She had the coffees, the fog was
right here, the tups were out on the in-bye with the ewes.
And Lori turns and looks back across the valley at their
little house and she thinks, the cat'll be curled up on her

chair, yes, that's how it'll be in there, and Lori crosses her fingers and says, for luck. We'll only have to wait until April for lambs.

LORI CROSSES THE GARBURN AND HEADS UP ONTO THE FELL

A good, steep climb to the top will get the warmth back into her, she thinks, and she looks to her left, to her right and she turns around and looks behind her. Light fog, she thinks, mist probably, and there are worse places to die than the bed, yes, if she's going to say anything on the matter that's what she'll say. It's where relaxed people die, Lori thinks, they let go of themselves, go too far with it and the old woman at the bus station clattered to the ground. There was something in her eyes that said she liked it that way, and well, Joseph's eyes are nothing like hers. He's got those heavy lids, as thick as blankets, yes, the effort it takes him to open them each morning. Shop-front shutters, she thinks, and thank God he went without making a spectacle of himself. Not a sound, Lori thinks, and she took another step towards the bed this morning. She hasn't done that since he woke with dead arms, months ago. And Lori thinks, quietly in, quietly out, yes, that's Joseph all over. She's the one who gets het up about things, small things, Joseph trying to get the lid off the honey jar for example, well, yes, that's a good example, she thinks, because struggling with a lid is hardly a crime, and Lori stops there on the steep fellside. Grip, then twist, she thinks, it's just grip then twist, and hasn't she always called his fingers fat? not fat, thick, Lori thinks, thick fingers and she makes herself guess when he jams them up inside her, left hand? right? and it's harder than you'd think, it's difficult to know what's going on down there. Although, wait. What's this she's saying? it's hardly as if it were only yesterday she was lying there on the bed guessing about hands and fingers, and it's fog, Lori thinks, far too dense to be called mist, and she pushes on up the steep fellside and she thinks she's done with bedroom activities. She's been done with them for years, yes, all that action has come down to nothing more than a peck on the cheek each night. That's what she gets and not every night either, no, he misses a few, and of course, he's right-handed, Joseph. Well, yes, she knew that, yes, she knows that. And she told herself a hundred times there was never going to be a baby, not with the pair of them carrying on, or not carrying on the way they were and once in a while she'd do it anyway, reach for the buckle on his belt, for the top button on his trousers.

N, n, n, no.

God, the stammer. She forgets about the stammer and then it comes fluttering right in as if it had never left. It's like a migratory bird, Lori thinks, a little pipit or something, and it's been ten long years since the Taylors left. At least, Lori thinks. And she stands there on the fellside and she pictures the tail-end of their yellow minibus disappearing down the lane. That was it, Lori thinks, over. And she says, Felix, Emile, Ross, Charlotte, Louise, Silas and she hears the smallest turn of wind at the grasses. Silas, Silas, Lori says. He'll almost be a man now, he'll be just about the same age Emile was the day he shot the crow down from the sky, a bit older maybe, and she thinks, go on up now, yes, push on up.

Definitely fog, she thinks, and she looks down and she sees
the peat, the black water around her boots. One step then
another step, she thinks, and she watches her feet go in and
out of the peat, she watches as the black water comes up
and falls away again and she thinks, not fog, clag, yes,
thicker than she's known it, and well, she can manage that
at least, she can keep an eye on where her feet are going,
and she looks down and she sees her leather boots and she
sees the line of peaty sediment just below the eyelets there
and she thinks, one foot then the other foot, one foot and
sooner or later she'll get to the summit. Although, no, it
isn't a summit, she thinks, it isn't anything grander than a
mound of tough grass with a handful of stones, and she
looks down at the black water around her boots, she looks
at the peat and the tufts of matgrass. Matgrass and soft
rush, she thinks, a blanket of bog moss, and she hears
Joseph saying, your boots'll ruin before long, love, and she
takes another step and she watches the black water come
up and fall away, and she still hasn't forgiven him. For
having a voice like an angel, she means. She can't begin to.
And Lori looks into the fog and she sees Joe kneeling down
next to the record player in the living room, she sees his
hair hanging down around his neck and she hears the
record going around on its turntable. The familiar sound of
dust and scratches, she thinks, and she looks over at Joe on
the floor down there and she sees how peaceful he looks,
and she thinks, lift the needle now Joe, because the music's
over, the music's finished, and bog mosses come in pinks
and oranges, in glassy greens, and all that heaviness about

him. His eyelids, his slippers, even his earlobes have thickened with age, she thinks, and then he opens his mouth. The place he sings from is so far from this world. It scarcely makes sense, Lori thinks. Purcell and Byrd, she thinks, Handel, Tallis, and he calls himself a countertenor, yes, everything that matters has a name. Apart from the cat, Lori thinks. The cat missed out, and already it feels like forever since she was there in the kitchen thanking God there wasn't a head, yes, she always thanks her lucky stars when there isn't a head, and why does she wait every morning? When the coffee's done, she means, why wait until it turns bitter? They've got themselves used to it now, the taste of coffee that's been sitting too long, and when she pushes open the bedroom door with her foot she's ready to say, at least it's been well-brewed, because it's become a bit of a joke between them, the coffee turning out as thick as tar and isn't it true? Lori thinks, isn't it true that every morning we're back to talking about the coffee? which is the way it is for most people, yes, everyone's more or less the same when it comes to the things they talk about, and they're late with the tups this year, we're already at the end of November and they've only just, she thinks. Heading for a cold spring then. April lambs and a cold spring. And Lori looks down at the black peat water, she watches as it comes up and falls away. And this last stretch across the top drags on. Isn't she always saying as much? And of course, Joe always says, not unlike Mahler 3 then.

Insufferable, Lori thinks, and she looks down at her boots and she sees the black water come up and fall away and she thinks, the fog is unusually dense, the fog is like, and she thinks, no, the fog is like nothing she knows, and Lori stops walking, she stands there on the broad top of the fell and looks down at the grasses and the swollen peat and she thinks, it never really stops raining around here. She gets tired of it, you get tired of it, coming down, coming down again, yes, everything between rains, Lori thinks, and at the end of a long winter she'll find herself standing at the kitchen window and with her hands together. *Agnus Dei*, she says. She doesn't know where she gets it from unless it's from *The Gazette*. Although it can't be. And some years the rain lets you alone for a week, two weeks, even. And then you're wishing it back, Lori thinks, God, yes, the rain is the oil in the system, and the day she lay her head back on the mound of tough grass at the top of the fell the sun had been hot for weeks, the peat had almost dried out, the needle-ends of the sedges were beginning to brown, and she thinks, walk a bit now Lori, keep moving, because she knows this last stretch drags on as long as a Mahler symphony, yes, but still, she'd expected to see the top a while back and Lori says, *Agnus Dei. Agnus Dei*, and she looks down at the swollen peat, at the black water around her boots and then into the fog, and there really isn't anything to be afraid of when it comes to fog, Lori thinks, no, it's nothing more than passing cloud.

Not really the wrong order, Lori thinks. You expect a parent
to go first, one parent then the other parent, which is how
it went with hers, and she hadn't really had time to get used
to the way things were before baby Fergus went too. Down
like dominoes all three, Lori thinks. And now Joe. Joe as
well. And she stands on the broad top of the fell and she
pictures all four of them laid out on the earth, one next to
the other. Like the war dead, she thinks, and she looks into
the fog and there isn't anything, and she looks down at
her boots, at the black water, the clumps of washed-out
matgrass and she remembers how small her mother looked
with the life gone out of her. It was as if she'd been an
illusion all along, Lori thinks, and she's never been able
to decide on the size of the gap between the living and the
dead. And well, no, she can't, she still can't. And she thinks
of baby Fergus lying dead and she thinks, at least Silas
didn't have to go. That's one small compensation, yes,
thanks be to God for that, she thinks, because she'd almost
got to know Silas that summer, she'd been watching him
pick daisies out on the lane since spring, since April or
thereabouts, and well, he can't have been older than seven,
eight at the most, Lori thinks. He'd gather up the daisies
and bring them back into the yard and then sit on the
ground by the woodpile and make them into chains. He'd
sit there slitting and threading for hours. She'd never seen
a patience like that on any of the other children. She'd
watched them all and she'd never seen anything approach-
ing it, Lori thinks. Almost preternatural. And she pictures
Silas slitting open stem after stem, she pictures the wedge
of green under his thumbnail and she thinks, you watched

him too closely, yes, she watched him the whole of that spring and summer and she's almost sure she'd never seen him run until the afternoon Emile got the air rifle from the shed and shot the crow. He ran well enough that day, Lori thinks, and she looks down at her boots and she thinks, there isn't even a proper cairn up at the top, no, there isn't anything more than a handful of stones and she's only going to get there by putting one foot down in front of the other, and she always says this stretch drags on. It's something to say, Lori thinks, and anyway she likes to hear Joe say, it won't drag on nearly as long as Mahler 3, love. Six movements of sheer tedium, he says, and she could more or less get across in her sleep. Fog or no fog, she thinks, clag or no clag, and she holds her hand up in front of her face and she sees it shaking and she takes another step.

Two shots, Lori thinks.

He got it on the second one, yes, the crow fell so slowly that everyone saw, Felix, Ross, Charlotte, Louise, Silas, and when Emile lowered the rifle he looked Silas in the eye, then cocked the gun a third time but the sky was already empty. Crows, rooks, jackdaws, swallows, all cleared out, Lori thinks, and she stood at the open window and watched as Silas ran out of the yard, down the bridleway and disappeared into the valley. She heard Emile say, little shit. Then he turned and spat, Lori thinks, a huge ball of it. And wasn't it almost hot that day, wasn't it almost sultry? And Lori tugs at the bottom of her jacket and well, yes, the cold's come in, she thinks, say it once and have done with it, and she looks down at her boots and she thinks, Silas ran all right, and she imagines him standing in the meadow at the bottom of the valley, she imagines him looking out into a sea of summer

grasses and she thinks, how did he ever find the crow in
there? Twenty minutes passed, yes, it was twenty minutes
at least before he made his way back up the bridleway with
the dead crow bundled in his T-shirt. He was so small. He
had the valley and the huge flank of the fell at his back,
but still, he walked up there with the crow against his chest
and those big strides boys take. And Lori remembers seeing
Silas on the lane, she remembers hearing the latch on the
gate slip out, slip back in again. Emile was hanging from
the woodpile roof. She remembers his long, lean muscles.
Emile is a man, she'd thought, the boy is almost all out
of him, and well, she sees the whole scene as if it happened
only yesterday or this morning, yes, she sees her scrawny
arms coming out from her sleeves, she sees Silas with the
dead crow, she sees Emile swing, let go.

And Emile looks Silas straight in the eye, yes, he keeps
his eyes fixed on Silas's eyes whilst he takes an imaginary
rifle up to the empty sky and jerks his arms back.

Bullseye, he says, and he spits again, but it isn't as big
and Silas walks over to the woodpile and puts the crow
down on top of the wood, the body before the head as if
the crow is only sleeping, yes, he leaves the crow on the
woodpile and walks over to Emile.

You tiny little prick, says Emile, and Lori turns and
sees the clouds coming in off the fells, although it's hot,
it's almost sultry still, and Lori thinks, look at those boys,
Silas and Emile, they're from the same stock. Yes, she really
sees it now, the same blood running through those boys,
and she watches as Emile turns and walks away from Silas,
a bouncing walk, Lori thinks, half-elastic, and she watches
as Silas runs up behind him. One, two, three, she counts,
and before she gets to four Silas kicks Emile in the back

of the knee and Lori watches as Emile falls down, as Silas kicks at his stomach, at his face and she stands at the open window and listens to the sound of Silas's shoes against Emile's body, six times she hears them and she hears Felix shout, Silas, Silas, she hears Charlotte, she hears Louise and she watches Silas kick. Behind him, she thinks, the valley, the huge flank of the fell.

And here comes Annie now. Lumbering still, Lori thinks. Weeks it's been going on, this lumbering, and well, it's about time the baby came out into the world, and she sees Annie lumbering across the yard in her flip-flops and she thinks, making a show of it, yes, look at that and she imagines the baby's head against the cervix, she thinks of its sticky hair, its screwed-up face, and she hears the sound of Silas's shoes against Emile's body and she thinks, surely it's time for the baby now, surely the time has come and gone. It has, she thinks, and she looks over and sees Annie pushing herself across the yard and she sees the baby already in Annie's arms and she thinks, my God, she thinks, dear God, because the baby is already here, yes, here it is at last, a tiny, living thing. A little lamb, yes, a precious little, Lori thinks, and she thinks, Dear God, *Agnus Dei*, and she hears Silas's shoes against Emile's body and she hears Annie's flip-flops pushing across the yard.

Boys, boys, Annie says, and her voice is like marble but she's lumbering, yes, the lumbering's still going on with her, Lori thinks, and she thinks, dear God, because she hadn't expected, no, she never really expects, and she thinks, this one will be the last at least. Seven is enough for anyone, Felix, Emile, Ross, Charlotte, Louise, Silas. And now a baby too, a little lamb, Lori thinks. With seven horns and seven eyes, and she never knows where she reads these things or if she dreams them up from nowhere and of course it's a boy, another little boy wrapped up there in blue, yes, first the crow and now the baby bundled up in blue and when it comes to babies nobody goes beyond seven, no, anything beyond seven isn't normal, Lori thinks, and she thinks, where's Paul? where's Paul now Silas is kicking at Emile and she thinks, already working away again, although hasn't it always been that way with him? yes, well, yes, she thinks, and she wipes the sweat from her face and she thinks, the heat won't last, no, we'll get to rain before the day's at its end, and Lori stands there at the open window and she sees Annie pass the sleeping baby to Felix and she thinks, the baby is as still as a doll. Its face is like plastic, or beeswax, and there. There, there, his body then his head in the crook of Felix's arm, and Lori holds her stomach. Straight to her stomach with the new babies, she thinks, and she's hardly been able to eat a thing of late. Still her belly always looks distended, yes, her belly makes her look as though she's six months gone, and she thinks, the body doesn't forget, the body's got a memory of its own, she thinks, and it's been eight years since Silas was born, you'd think that'd be long enough to get over this thing she has about babies, and she looks at Felix standing there in the yard with the baby sleeping in his arms, she looks at Annie crouching next to Emile. Her summer dress and flip-flops. All her children, Lori thinks.

It drags on, she thinks, yes, isn't she always saying? and it'll
be months yet until they get a day as warm as the day Emile
shot the crow. You can go a whole summer without a day
like that, a hot day, a sultry day, Lori thinks. Silas had been
playing out in the yard in his shorts for weeks and it was
only when he came back up from the valley with the dead
crow in his T-shirt that she noticed the clouds coming in off
the fells, and well, she's got that day stuck in her head now,
yes, she can run right through that day from beginning to
end, from the moment Emile came out of the shed with the
air rifle to the moment she let herself look down into baby
Fergus's basket, and Lori thinks, Fergus, no, and she feels
something open up inside her stomach. Something like
a hand, she thinks, or a flower, and she'd promised herself,
yes, she'd more or less vowed that she wouldn't get tangled
up with the seventh one, yes, the moment she found out
another baby was on its way she bent over the last of the
courgettes out there in the veg patch. She held her hands
together. Not this one, she said. *Agnus Dei*, she said, *Agnus*,
Agnus, *Dei*, and the courgettes were huge. She'd left them
so long they'd grown tough skins, big seeds, and well, she
could always start again with the yard, Lori thinks. It's
never too late in the year to dig over the soil, yes, you can
always turn the soil or spend a bit of time getting rid of
stones, and baby Fergus, baby Fergus, it wasn't exactly her
fault, no, Annie should have been done with babies after
Silas. You'd expect anyone to be done with all that after six,
Lori thinks, and the day Emile shot the crow Lori watched
from the open window as Annie came lumbering, babe
in arms, and she thinks, it's always the stomach with these

things, yes, she'd felt something give deep inside her and
Lori pictures herself standing at the window, her stomach
opening itself up into a hollow bamboo and she thinks,
always the stomach, or behind the eyes, although she
couldn't say where exactly and Lori looks down at her
boots, at the drops of water settled on the smooth stems
of rush and she thinks, miles to go.

And it's fair to say that everyone starts from the same place.
You have one baby and go up from there, although of course
Annie had twins, Felix and Emile, and she thinks, get over
it at last, Lori, because Felix and Emile will be almost thirty
now, Felix and Emile will be more or less the same age she
was the day they moved in, and she doesn't like to think of
time preying on children, no, there's something awful, she
thinks, and she looks down at her boots, at the black peat
water and she thinks, it's been twenty-five years, twenty-
five and a half years since she first set eyes on them. They
were toddlers, only two or three or years old, she thinks.
Their lives the size of their little yard, and she thinks of
Felix and Emile out in the yard with their trucks and their
spades, she thinks of them under a huge white sky, in the
last of the evening light and in the early morning cold,
under the rain, the sun, shorts and trousers, knitted jumpers, red and green and brown and grey and coats, wellies,
mud, dust, stones. She thinks of all the endless afternoons.
That feeling when they'd finished for the day, she thinks.
A jumper abandoned on the laurel, a tractor and a truck
parked in the sandpit. As if it would all go on indefinitely.
New mornings with trucks and sticks and mud and she
thinks, take another step or two, and she looks into the
thick fog and she thinks, the boys were out there so early

some mornings. Two pairs of royal blue wellies and their
voices carrying like birdsong, up and in through the
bedroom window, and Joseph would turn over in bed and
say, not now, say, can't you get them to shut up, Lo?

It was glorious, she thinks. We were glorious. And she
takes a step and she takes another step and she pictures
herself lying in bed next to Joe, she pictures her hands on
his bare back. He's always been so warm-blooded, she
thinks, whenever he staggered out to the bathroom in
the night she'd curl up in the empty space. She's the cold
one, yes, she's the one who wears socks in bed. Angora,
she thinks, although not back then. She's got cold. And she
thinks, can't you get them to shut up, Lo? all his freedom
gone in one jab of the penis. Think of that, Lo, one foul jab
and you end up with twins.

That's exactly what he said, Lori thinks, word for word,
then he pulled his arms out from under the duvet and took
her head in his hands and whispered, thank God, Lo, just
you and me. Tea for two and two for tea, and she'd almost
melted into him. And Lori thinks, huge white skies and
evening rains that played through the night, and she thinks,
too much music and too much rain. By morning she could
hardly tease them apart, and she looks down at the peat, at
the rushes and the grasses and she thinks, the sun comes
out of nowhere. It always happens, even in late November
it happens, and he held her head in his hands and she'd
thought, give him time, give us time.

And well, she curses herself now, yes, she sees herself
for what she was, and she thinks, a silly little girl. Couldn't
see the wood for the trees, and she would have been far
better off ripping his precious penis out from inside his
Y-fronts and well, she wouldn't have any trouble finding

the hole, the fly, these days. God knows she's washed and dried his Ys often enough and half the time she'll find one of her fingers slipping through that slit and she thinks, does it really need to be that big? because she can hardly imagine, no, well, no, she doesn't like to imagine, and she thinks, little tractors and trucks, blues and browns and greys and she thinks, one foul jab. And she got out of bed and walked the few steps over to the window. She looked out across the valley at the fell. Coffee? she said, and well, she does more or less the same thing every morning.

LORI PUTS HER HAND OUT TO TOUCH THE PILE OF STONES

Thank God, she thinks, because this last stretch really drags on, yes, isn't she always saying, doesn't she always say? and she's been up here for hours or what feels like hours, and Lori puts her hand out and touches the stones and she thinks, they never seem like enough. Let the fell carry itself, she thinks, and one day in summer, maybe two or three summers ago she put her head back on the grass at the top here, she shut her eyes and fell asleep. She's only ever done it once in her life, fallen asleep under a blue sky. There wasn't a sound that day, there wasn't anything more than the sound she mistakes for the wind sometimes. And Lori sits down on the damp grass at the top of the fell, she pulls up her hood and rests her head back against the grass.

After a while she hears the light, suspended there in the fog, and she thinks, the ears will tell you as much as the eyes if you let them, yes, she spends too much time on the eyes these days, and she opens her mouth and the fog slides in and slides out again and she thinks if she liked any of Joseph's records at all it was the Duruflé. Duruflé, with its voices climbing like stone walls, and she lets the fog slide in and she thinks, miles and miles of wall, and ghosts of working hands in every stone, and of course she hears what she wants to hear with the Duruflé. The sounds of home, she thinks, the web of stone walls running over the fells, yes, threads and filaments under a thick white sky and she thinks, of all skies it's the most familiar. And she lets the fog slip in, slip out again and if anything the familiar's more overwhelming than the unfamiliar, she thinks, because what does it really mean to know the fell, the sky,

the way she does? And she thinks, an early December sun
brings yellow light, a Uranian blue sky, and she looks into
the fog and she thinks, they're still there, Great End, Great
Gable, Great Rigg, Red Screes, Morecambe Bay, and it's the
only place she can think of where she feels the right size.
The house, the car, the phone and its little semi-circular
table, all of them make her feel far too big. Yes, she likes to
compare herself to the fell, she likes to feel herself return
to her rightful size and she pictures herself pushing at
the bedroom door with her foot and she thinks, there's
nowhere to go.

And Lori sits on top of the fell and she hears the light
suspended there in the fog, a late November light, she
thinks. And if she's got to live in a tiny house she wants it
quiet. The last thing she wants is music. Go and sit in the
car if you want music, she thinks, and well, he does, yes, he
already does and she thinks, it's been years since she heard
him sing and if his voice has set as thick as his face she'll
never know, and she thinks, who cares? No, she couldn't
care, because all she manages to think when she sees him
open his mouth out there is shut up. That's the best she
can do before getting herself out of earshot, and she thinks,
the ears are as much a problem as the eyes, and she lets the
fog slip in and out and in again and she thinks of the long
thread of wall running up from the Kentmere Valley. At
some point it just ends, she thinks, and she sits herself up
and she thinks, eat something now, yes, get some food
down you and she holds her hand out in front of her and
she thinks, put the hand away, yes, out of sight, she thinks,
because she can't stomach seeing a hand that won't behave.
A wobbling head is easier on the nerves than a wobbling
hand, and she'll have one of those scones now. She hasn't

had so much as a mouthful all day, and well, if she hadn't
been in such a hurry this morning she could have had
Joseph's coffee, God, yes, another coffee would have kept
the warmth in a bit longer, and anyway she likes a second
mug, hasn't she always liked a second mug? And Lori
thinks, eat the scone. Get it down you, although she hardly
feels hungry, no, a scone's the last thing she wants really.
They're so dry. And well, she can see why Joseph was after
the honey last night. You need a bit of moisture, yes, you'll
never swallow them down without a bit of help, and she'd
heard him in the kitchen, she'd thought, grip and twist, why
don't you just grip then twist? and she's so predictable, isn't
she, there aren't any surprises in here, Lori thinks, and she
goes to tap her head, but no, she doesn't want to go scuffing
at her head with a shaking hand when what she really needs
is a sharp tap. And he can't have been feeling too bad when
he went for the scone last night. He got up from the sofa
and shuffled into the kitchen the way he usually does. Grip,
then twist. Grip. And here she goes. Joseph's thick fingers,
yes, that's what's she's coming to, and well, she can't leave
it at fingers, can she? She doesn't let go easily and she
thinks, too thick, and he shoves a bit when he puts them
inside her, yes, he gives a little shove to get them up where
he wants them. She lines up her teeth, she brings her jaw
so far forward her cheek twitches, and she'll have a scone
now, and Lori puts her hand into her jacket pocket and she
feels her hand shaking and she thinks, keep the fuck, will
you? and well, she can't, no, she can't, and she feels that the
scones have more or less crumbled in there. Already stale,
she thinks, if they're crumbling like that and every time
Joseph puts his fingers inside her he tells her she feels so
good, mmm. He makes the same noise when he brings fish

and chips up from town, two large cod, and Lori thinks, mmm, mmm, and well, she can't expect him to reinvent the wheel every time he opens his mouth. It isn't as if he's the only one repeating himself. She does it all the time, the whole bloody time and it hardly matters what goes in there, fingers, fist, penis. She can't tell one from the other once it's in. And he gives a little shove to get himself up, mmm.

No, don't, no. N, n, n, no.

Because she gave up on that years ago, going for the buckle on his belt, she means, and well, she can hardly go near his Ys these days without thinking of things that lurch or bob. Koi carp, celery in a casserole. And she thinks, not that as well, because she likes celery, yes, she enjoys a bit of celery if it isn't too stringy, and she thinks, a stove-pipe sponge eats almost anything that passes. A huge, hungry tube. And how can she know something like that when she won't read anything that isn't *The Gazette*? The books smell, she thinks, of mould, she thinks, and all she ever got in return for her fumblings was a

D, d, don't.

And she feels herself breathing, she feels her chest pushing out and sucking in and she thinks, relax, just relax because it's all over, yes, everything's done, and if she's told herself once she's told herself a thousand times, there's nothing to be got from poking around in old wounds. There's nothing but misery to be found, she thinks, and the day Emile shot the crow, which was weeks before baby Fergus died, all she'd wanted was to look. And she thinks, looking at a baby is hardly a crime, and she goes to rub her eyes and she thinks, stop with the eyes now, the eyes are fine.

And Annie must have asked Felix to take baby Fergus back inside, yes, that's what must have happened that day, because Felix had Fergus in the crook of his arm and a few minutes later he walked across the yard towards the house and went in through the back door. And if it isn't the stomach she doesn't know where. No, she doesn't know where it is for disappointment. Not the eyes. The eyes are for sadness, for despair, and she thinks, you can't isolate, stop isolating. The babies always came out bouncing anyway, yes, she could only get herself so far with hoping for an infection to take hold or a placenta to separate. For a cleft palate or a cleft hand. Hydrocephalus, spina bifida, and all in all she deserved them, her whittled-down hips, her globy knees, because what sort of person prays for a baby born dead? And here she is on the top of the fell with a fistful of crumbs. Get them down you, she thinks, eat the sodding crumbs and go home, and she pictures Felix walking back out into the yard without the baby, and well, she took a few more minutes at the window then slipped on her shoes and stepped out into the lane. There were foxgloves on the bank, yes, the bank was pink and purple.

Lori stands outside the Taylors' front door and she thinks, get yourself on inside then, and she reaches out, pushes down on the door handle and steps up into the porch.

It smells, she thinks. It smells of leeks or cabbages or something in here, and she turns to shut the door behind her. No, she thinks, leave it open a crack, and she pulls the door until the light falls to a slit. Yes, she thinks, good, and she walks on into the living room. Two sofas. Two sofas and two armchairs, she thinks. And she looks at the photos on the walls and she looks at the photos on the mantelpiece, Felix and Emile, Ross and Charlotte and Louise and she sees that with Silas the smile comes from his mouth.

All the others smile from the eyes, Lori thinks, especially Louise, yes, Louise is a happy one, and she looks down and sees how thin the carpet is beneath her feet, and another thin patch over there by the door to the stairs, she thinks. It's almost as bad as ours. And well, she wouldn't have thought, no, you don't think, and Lori crosses the living room and opens the wooden door that leads to the stairs, she stands on the bottom step and looks up. Go on up then, she thinks, and she feels the cold coming off the walls, and well, she knows it takes the best part of summer for these old houses to warm up. Theirs is the same, yes, by the time winter comes around again the walls are carrying that skin of water. Like ice, Lori thinks, and she walks on up between the two cold walls, and she thinks, when was the last time? no, she can't remember the last time she saw all the Taylor children in the yard together.

Silas bolted, she thinks, he kicked like a colt. And she's spent all these months half-hoping for something like an umbilical cord around the baby's neck, although not really, no, it isn't quite like that, and Lori gets to the top of the stairs and walks along the landing. Seven, she thinks. Seven, seven, once you start counting you can see that it's hardly normal and she thinks, two sofas. Two sofas and two armchairs, and she thinks, don't torture yourself and she pushes at one of the doors and looks in and sees that the baby's basket is on the floor next to the bed, yes, a little Moses basket down there in the shade and she thinks, little darling, precious little. And isn't she the one who turns off the light at night and prays for blue skin, for blood to pool at little lips? Isn't she always praying for things to get as bad as they can get? And she thinks, dear God, because all she wants is some respite, yes, she has to keep herself afloat somehow. You have to keep going, she thinks, and she breathes in deeply and whatever the smell is it isn't leeks. Not leeks after all, she thinks, and she walks across the room, she steps around the bed and over to the basket. Not yet, she says, and she goes on over to the window and looks out into the yard and across the valley, and she thinks, the same valley, the same fell.

And it'll rain. We've been waiting on rain, Lori says, and she stands at the window and she sees the thick green bracken covering the fellside, she sees tiny dots of pink and purple and she thinks, there's no stopping it, this thing we're spinning. Lines and threads, she thinks, and she looks over at the basket and she thinks, the baby is already part of this. Nobody gets to turn back. Not Emile, not Silas, not the crow, and she looks at Silas down there in the yard with the dead crow on his knee and she looks at Emile and she thinks, the blood's still coming, still flowing, and Lori presses her face against the windowpane and breathes out until the window fogs up and she thinks, two sofas. Two sofas and two armchairs and she'd be wrong to think it's a bed of roses for Annie. Paul works away half the time, yes, it's half the time at least with him, Lori thinks, and Annie's said it herself, he leaves her the tail end. Washing, cooking, cleaning, shopping, it goes round and round for Annie, it's a never-ending trail of cups and plates and socks, and thank God he got them the microwave, yes, she's said it enough times, the microwave's transformed things. Once she'd got herself over the taste, yes, she had to get herself over that, but it means the older boys can fend for themselves a bit. Even Emile will stick a potato in the microwave and turn the dial, and the window's fogged up, Lori thinks, and she turns around and sees the basket there on the floor next to the bed, yes, the little Moses basket there in the shade and she thinks, the baby is really here, yes, once you're here, she thinks, and it'll rain. All night probably, yes, it all goes by, she thinks, and she crouches down next to the basket.

She didn't kill him by looking. No, it's madness to say it's her fault when there isn't any fault to be had. Although she'll wager the eyes haven't forgiven her because it's every morning now with the eyes. She brought it on herself, yes, she crouched down next to the basket. He was wrapped in his blanket, he was a bale of hay with a little head, and she brought her own head so close she heard him breathing. He didn't need much air at all, Lori thinks, nothing but air and milk and hardly any and she listened to his tiny ins and outs, she couldn't take her ears off him, the ears, she thinks, not the eyes, and she'll say outright that she's never seen a thing so poor. So helpless, she means, because a newborn lamb will always try to stand. A strong northerly and it'll still try, and the wind was pushing the clouds across the sky, there were threads, she thinks, too many threads, bracken and foxgloves and she'd hung her head over his basket, a tiny boy, a precious little and she hadn't wanted anything more than to be found, yes, if someone had just found us, she thinks, because she was bent right over his tiny breaths, she was far too close.

It must have been the rain that jolted her out of it, the rain or the sound of the boys laughing out there in the yard, yes, she'd stood herself up and said, we're already done then, you and me. Out of time already. And well, she never really says the right thing, no, she hardly ever says anything that's actually worth saying.

Which is what always happens, yes, the rain went on all
evening and through the night and by mid-morning it was
down to drizzle, dry enough to get out into the yard and
pull a few weeds, yes, she likes to get to the weeds after a
good rain, although the soil clumps. There are worse things,
Lori thinks, you can bash off a bit of sticky soil with a fork,
yes, a nice two-tine fork does the job on the weeds and
she must have been ready for Annie and the baby, she must
have been half-waiting, she thinks, and she does it to
herself, yes, you still do it to yourself Lori Fitzgerald.

And Lori pushes the fork into the earth. A strong jab before
lifting, she thinks. Then firmly grasp. Yes, jab then grasp,
and Lori pulls the weed from the earth and she looks
across the yard and she thinks, already, yes, she's only been
out here a matter of minutes and already. And Lori sees
Annie crossing the yard with the baby in her arms, and if
she isn't a bit lighter on her feet today, Lori thinks, yes,
already losing the lumbering and she thinks, a strong jab,
and she spears the fork into the earth and a small round
of congratulations will do the trick, yes, a quick congratulations, and she pulls the weed from the earth and knocks
at the dirt with the tines, and, yes.

Congratulations, congratulations to you, Lori says.

He's here at last, arrived, Annie says, if you want to have
a little look. And Lori stands up and looks down at the baby.

Yes, congratulations all round, she says.

Meet little Fergus, Annie says.

Yes, Fergus, hello, and doesn't he look a bit like Silas,
Silas more than any of the others?

Silas? Annie says, and she tilts the baby's face towards
Lori and says, here, look, and Lori looks at the baby and
well, she's got the fork and the weed, yes, she's standing
here with the weed, the weed and the fork.

Congratulations then, Lori says, and she throws the
weed behind her and she says, it's easier after a good rain,
with the weeds, although the soil clumps, and well, yes,
it does, she thinks, it really sticks and she should have got
to the weeds weeks ago, the place is overrun, she thinks,
and she says, yes, yes, congratulations then, congratulations, and she doesn't know why she said that. There isn't
any need for more congratulations, no, she should be done
with congratulations by now, and well, Annie is already
talking about all the commotion yesterday, about Silas
and Emile, and I'll tell you where I found that crow this
morning. In the chicken shed, that's where I found it, and
not much of it because the chickens had had a good go
and Lord only knows what Silas was doing in there, a law
unto himself that boy, and don't they always say you've got
to expect a difficult one? isn't there always a difficult one?
Fingers crossed then, Annie says, fingers crossed there
won't be any trouble with little Fergus here, and she draws
her thumb across the baby's forehead.

And Lori says, no, no, there's enough trouble around
without trouble from that one, and now, Lori says, I'm off
inside to peel some veg, and she gestures towards the
kitchen door with her weeding fork and she says, if we're
having casserole tonight, yes, it's about time I got started
on the veg, and Lori sees Annie nodding, but no, it's hardly
interesting, is it, going on in to peel veg? no, it's boring,
Lori thinks, peeling veg and making a casserole, it's hardly
a thing to talk about over the garden fence, not now there's

another new baby, no, next to a newborn baby a casserole is nothing, and Lori hears Annie singing, yes, a little whisper of a song in the baby's ear and Lori thinks, let her sing. If Joe's allowed his Duruflé then Annie can have her song, yes, Annie can have her *Sunshine, my only sunshine* and Lori gestures towards the kitchen door with her weeding fork. I'm off inside to do the veg then, she says, peel the potatoes at any rate, and it won't hurt to make a big pot, to make enough for all of yours if you'd like. A big pot never hurts. And Lori says, it'll give you a break from the cooking, no, you shouldn't have to be worrying about cooking now the baby's arrived, and if I'm not mistaken there's a spare casserole dish floating around somewhere in there, it's got a hairline crack but we use it, it doesn't do any worse than any other dish we've got going, and it can't hurt, no, it won't hurt to peel a few more carrots, a few more potatoes, there's enough veg in there to feed an army, if that's what they say. And now she's laughing, yes, that's what she's doing, laughing about veg, about making a casserole and it's hardly interesting, going on about casseroles and veg, but she can hear herself doing it anyway, going on and on about veg, and she gestures at the door with her two-tine fork and she hears herself saying, carrots, onions, potatoes, celery, she hears herself saying, no trouble at all, not a bit, no, and she thinks, how long can you talk about veg, how long can you go on and on about veg when you look like you haven't eaten in a month, a year?

And Annie says, no, really, we'll eat you out of house and home. It's the boys, it's Felix, Emile, even Ross, Annie says, you couldn't begin to imagine where they put it all, and she looks down into the baby's eyes and she says, nothing but milk for you, and long may it last and Lori says, yes, milk, congratulations, and is she half stupid or something, going on and on with her congratulations? And she gestures towards the back door with her weeding fork and she hears herself saying, too many potatoes anyway, we can't eat our way through those sacks that Joe buys, you'll be doing us a favour, you'll be doing me a favour at any rate because nothing feels worse than throwing out veg. And Annie says, well, if you really don't mind, if it really isn't any trouble and she says, oh, wait, wait, take Fergus a moment because look, and Lori looks and she sees Louise up there on the woodpile roof and Annie shouts, hold on a moment, hold on there Lou, and Lori bends down and jabs the weeding fork into the soil and holds her arms out to take the baby.

No mum, Louise says, I can do it. And Annie says, slowly then, be careful Lou, and Louise slides, then jumps.

False alarm everyone, relax, Annie says. False alarm and yet another pair of soaking wet jeans, and Lori stands by the small fence with her arms out in front of her and she thinks, put your arms down you stupid cow, if you don't want to look like a weeding fork yourself, and she thinks, dear God, because her arms won't go down, and she thinks, can you just, well, can you? And she sees Annie walking away, walking over to Louise and she thinks, still lumbering then, although not really, no, and she thinks, put the arms down, the arms aren't needed, and she doesn't know whether to make a big pot or not, because it'll mean peeling an awful lot of veg, yes, she'll be tied to the kitchen sink all afternoon if she's got to peel enough veg for a family that size.

If she isn't including the old woman at the bus station, which she isn't, no, she's already decided on that and five's too many anyway. Five's on the other side of normal, Lori thinks, and she can't sit up here all day counting the dead, no, she'll need to get on if she wants to be home before dark, and well, yes, she does want to be home before dark, or at least off the fell, God, yes, the last thing she wants is to be picking her way down here in the dark and she thinks, get up and get on then, and she looks into the fog and she thinks, what day is it anyway? the twenty-fifth, the twenty-sixth of November? The year's almost done, and she thinks, the twenty-sixth, if the bins went out yesterday, although it could easily have been the day before with the bins, and she thinks, one day merges into another. You wait for your sliver of light, she thinks.

And she'll say it was last night, yes, for the sake of argument she'll say it was last night after Joe had gone up, that she'd resolved to do something about the bike, about the *LeMond*, and she thinks, if you want to say *Chambéry* then say it, let the *r* come out the way it wants to and she sits on the mound of grass up there on top of the fell and she says, *Chambéry* and she looks into the fog and she waits to feel something, and she thinks the *Chambéry* is hardly the problem she's made it out to be. It's been leaning up against the kitchen table for so long she scarcely registers it anymore, yes, she's happy enough to make the little trip around its back wheel to get to the pedal bin. The only way out is backwards, Lori thinks, yes, how many times does a person need to reverse out of a tight space before getting used to it? And she'd waited until he'd gone upstairs to bed before pouring herself a drop of Merlot. Me*r*lot, she thinks, and she listens to the *r* and she waits to feel something and she thinks, the cheeks for shame, although it flushes up from the chest on a bad one, and she'd poured the Merlot recklessly, she'd let it splash and slosh. The house can't cope, she thinks. The whole kitchen throbs with noise after something like that and she'd heard Joseph shuffle to the top of the stairs.

What was that, love?

And she'd thought, fuck off. Fuck back off to bed. No, she can't bring another word out of herself once he's gone up. And now he's dead, Lori thinks. The fourth one. And well, that answers that question, doesn't it, the question of who will die first, and it wasn't her, no, she's the winner, if you can call it that, because by all accounts going on is harder than dying, if you die quickly, and well, a lot depends on that, she thinks, yes, a lot of life's worries would fizzle out with the promise of a swift death and it was just like Joseph to slip neatly away. Like a snake, like a taipan, she thinks. There was nothing, not even the sound of his yellow underbelly gliding over the sand, and this thing with the *Chambéry* has gone on too long, yes, the *Chambéry*'s outstayed its welcome at our table, Lori thinks, and she supposes it's her fault, yes, she's the one who lets things drag on around here, she's the one who takes the little trip around the back wheel without so much as a squeak. All those extra steps, she thinks, and of course the *Chambéry*'s just the tip of the iceberg, the sum of all those parts she keeps finding around the house. Components, she means, because he really has been going too far with all that, brake callipers, speed shifters, a rear derailleur on the bread bin. The rear cassettes in the outside loo. And she'd poured herself a glass of Merlot, she'd made up her mind to wait until morning before starting on the *Chambéry*, because in all these years they haven't ever gone to bed on an argument, no, she can't ever remember a cross word before bed.

And thank God he's given up explaining, she thinks, because she's never exactly been interested in how a chain moves between sprockets, how a rear derailleur maintains a light tension. He could be an awful lot worse when it comes to going on.

Everything has a job to do, everything has a function, love, although he won't go on, no, he never says too much, he isn't the type, and it can't be more than a few days ago that she slipped on a copy of *Cranked*. It seemed quite funny, Lori thinks, for a man of Joseph's age to leave a copy of *Cranked* on the floor next to the bed, and she'd meant to have a little joke, yes, she'd meant to lighten things up between them because they haven't ever gone so far they can't find room for a laugh or two, and well, all things considered there have been a lot of jokes in our little house, yes, it's difficult to imagine getting as far along as we have without laughing, Lori thinks, and she thinks of Joseph lying dead on the bed and she thinks, well yes, that's what you come to in the end.

IT ISN'T THE FIRST TIME SHE'S DONE IT, PASSED THE DAMP OFF AS COLD

How long do you actually need, Lori thinks, before it even registers? because for all she knows she's been sitting up here for close to an hour, and nothing, nothing beyond a vague spreading feeling. And Lori stands up and peels her trousers away from her skin. It isn't exactly straightforward, she thinks, finding the line between cold and damp, if it actually is a line, and well, the point is that every time she brings a basket of washing in from the back room she squeezes at the sleeves of Joe's woollens thinking, cold or damp? damp or cold? And no, she can't tell, not until she's let them sit in the warm awhile. And she doesn't know why she bothers hanging anything in the back room, let alone his woollens. There's no real way back with them. If you've hung them once, she means. And she doesn't know why she does, hang them out the back there. It's hardly the ideal environment for drying things. Nothing dries, she thinks, even in summer, even when she leaves the sliding door open. The air doesn't circulate, no, the air doesn't seem to, she thinks, and the washing line itself is pocked with mould, but she hangs anyway. Vests and Ys mostly, because if anything's going to dry, she thinks, and she'd get one of those plastic-coated lines, she'd get one in red or metallic blue, but who's going to put that up, she thinks, because they don't, no, we don't seem to, and if he wants his woollens lying flat he can find somewhere to lay them. Yes, do it yourself, love, she says, and she hears her voice arrive and depart, and she looks down at her boots then into the fog and she says, do it yourself, love, do-it-your-self. And where did it come from, this habit she has, of saying things out loud, of announcing things? and she thinks, it isn't where, it's why, yes, why's the question she should be asking herself, and well, it's company of sorts, yes, it's a reminder, that she's not alone, although she is alone, yes, she knows she's alone and she looks down at her boots and she sees a little crack in the leather, she sees it running across the big toe. Like a river delta, she thinks, like one of those aerial photographs you get, and she thinks, yes, you get them, aerial photographs of water and sediment and it's hardly unusual, she thinks, saying a few words to yourself here and there, everybody's got something. Even Joe, and well, she forgets, doesn't she? She forgets the stammer until she hears him pecking away at his Ds and Ns. Although when was the last time? when was it really? Lori thinks, and she peels her trousers away from her skin and she thinks, the stammer's probably gone by now. Didn't he always say it was a young man's problem, wasn't that his line? And she's let the cold come in, although only as far as the hands, yes, that's where she feels it, and Lori claps her hands together and she hears the sound of her clapping stop dead.

Walk on over to Sallows then, Lori thinks, yes, pushing on can only be better than turning back, which almost never feels good. And she looks into the fog and she thinks, it won't rain, no, Sallows then up on to Yoke, if the light's still holding, and Joe went to bed early last night. It hardly registered when he said he was unusually tired, if he did say that, Lori thinks, and well, this is how things are with us these days, we're like ships in the night, that's all we have left say to each other, we're like ships in the night, aren't we, love? But no, that isn't what we're like, it's easy to say ships in the night and it's an excuse, Lori thinks, because when he's asleep she slips on in behind him.

We've always been such a good fit, she thinks, which was a surprise to begin with, Lori being Lori and Joe being Joseph Charles from the School of Music, and she thinks, perhaps it was the *Royal* School of Music, which would make our fitting even more unlikely, and once she's sure he's sleeping she slips on in behind him. She pulls hairs from the back of his head, she just pulls them, one, two, as many as seven. It's as if nothing's been taken, Lori thinks, and she shakes her left leg and she shakes her right leg and she thinks, come down off the top here, pick up the wall at Moor Head, and she walks down off the top, she comes down a few paces, thirty, thirty-five maybe, and she turns and looks back and there isn't anything. Already nothing, she thinks. You only need a half-clear day to see this little mound of grass from the top of Sallows, from the top of Yoke, of Ill Bell probably, which is a good three miles from here as the crow flies, and she thinks, get yourself as far as Moor Head, then decide. Go on up or turn back. And she thinks, go on, because the way she feels now she could walk all day, yes, she's so happy when she's walking, she feels it somewhere near her heart. It spreads outwards, she thinks, yes it's almost the whole body for happiness, and she thinks, pick up the wall at Moor Head, go up on to Yoke. Take the ridge along to Froswick if you want, and she looks down at her boots, at the grasses and sedges, and it was only last week or the week before she was telling Joe that the bracken will need cutting back if they want to see any colour on the fellside come spring. What's that, love? he said, and she said, the bracken, love, and she said, don't worry love, I might just fix up a round of sandwiches with that cooked ham, if you've got a bit of space, and Lori looks down at her boots and she thinks they'll need to do something with the bracken if they don't want it taking over the fellside. Give it ten years, give it one hundred years, and she thinks, come on down off the top here and cross the moor at least, and she hears her boots against the grass, she hears them on the sodden earth, over and over she hears them and she thinks, come down here, drop the gentle fifty feet or so. And Lori thinks, fifty familiar feet, yes, even in the clag the place is as familiar as a hand, a face, and she thinks, whose face? and Lori thinks, his heavy lids, it's as though he's never woken up, and she feels the earth beneath her, she feels it give and return. A little patch of floating bog, she thinks, and she looks down and she knows, yes, this little patch here, and another just past Moor Head. Familiar ground, and she thinks, push on then. Get on if you're going on.

A clean knife there, love, she'd said. For your Dijon, if you're wanting Dijon with that ham, and Lori sees herself standing in the kitchen, she sees herself wiping her hands down the front of her old apron, she sees its thick navy and white stripes. If you're wanting it, love, the Dijon, for that ham, she says. I'll put it back if not, and she stands there on the sodden earth and she sees the sandwich sitting on the plate, and she sees the clean knife lying next to the pot of Dijon and she thinks, the ham's never good cold anyway, it flakes, and she feels the chill around her middle and she thinks, push on then, if you're going on, and she'll not get up onto Yoke after all. Given the light, she thinks, no, she shouldn't be considering anything beyond Sallows at this time of day and Lori looks into the fog and she thinks, Colman's would do. She pays over a pound for Dijon. He gets through it, yes, he'll normally, she thinks, and she

69

walks on over the moor and she thinks, pick up the wall, then decide, because she can always come back down on the Garburn, yes, she can always pick up the Garburn at the Nook. Then home, Lori thinks, and she pushes on over the sodden earth and she thinks, if you'll get yourself as far as the wall, if you'll just get yourself, and she hears a noise out there in the fog.

Not alone then, Lori thinks, and Lori looks down at her boots and she sees the little crack running across the big toe. She'll have to get some neatsfoot into the leather if she wants another winter out of them, and well, yes, she does. The miles it takes to break in a new pair, she thinks, and she takes a few steps over the sodden earth. Matgrass and soft rush and all these bog mosses she can't name, no, she can't begin to, and she hears the noise again, she hears the raven croaking somewhere out there in the fog and she thinks, nothing more than a massive crow. Massive nonetheless, yes, a raven can make a buzzard look small, even the shadow of a raven, she thinks, and no, no, she didn't murder him, she didn't lay a hand, not so much as a finger and she goes to rub her eyes and she thinks, the eyes are OK, the eyes clear themselves if you give them half a chance, and she pushes her boots over the rough ground and she thinks, the shadow of a raven? no, she hasn't ever, you don't ever, and she hears the raven somewhere out there in the fog. Over there, she thinks, by Ewe Crags already and she'll eat something now, yes, a couple of mouthfuls will be better than nothing and she looks at her pocket and she sees the two scones bulging and she thinks, no, she can't really face anything right now, not even a digestive, although she'll normally, and Lori pushes her boots over the rough ground and she thinks, it'll be the small packets from now on then, if she wants digestives in the house, she means, yes, she'll have to work to get through even a small packet before they go soft. Two with her afternoon tea, she thinks, yes, she'll manage an extra digestive if she pushes supper back half an hour, and she thinks, dear God, fretting about digestives when she'll more than likely be filling up the bin with bread, with potatoes, and she thinks she'll never have a marrow in the house again, no, a marrow's too overwhelming for one. A marrow's almost too overwhelming for two, and she thinks, marrow soup, roasted marrow. She's even gone as far as marrow and ginger jam. Nobody really wants marrow jam, she thinks, and well, she can forget about marrows until summer, although it isn't just, no, not just, Lori thinks, it's cabbages and pumpkins, it's cauliflowers, it's broccoli, lettuces. Especially lettuces because she only eats the outer leaves. The inner ones don't taste, and she thinks, Joe'll take anything, Pot Noodle even, and whatever those little rectangles are he puts in the toaster, and when it comes to opening a can he'll say, the biggest half for me, love, and she thinks, no more tuna either, no, she'd rather stop with tuna altogether than have a half-can festering in the fridge. You can't, she thinks, and she puts her hand into her pocket and she thinks, later, wait a bit with the scones, and she looks down at her boots and she looks into the fog and she thinks, a dog would help her out with a few soft digestives, yes, a dog would solve a lot of the problems with food. She'll go on over to the farm in the morning then, or even this after-noon, if she gets back in the light, and if they haven't got a litter over there she'll ask old John where else she can try because she hasn't had a dog since, and she thinks, since Big Ranulph.

And Lori thinks, a new start, yes, she can get the *Chambéry* out to the shed and then she'll put a couple of old blankets down under the table and she thinks, there's nothing bad in a dog, nothing that's gone bad, she means, and she looks down at her boots and she hears them tread onto the sodden earth, again and again she hears them and she thinks, creeping bent, common bent, velvet bent, and she listens to her boots and she thinks, this is it then, nothing more, which is a whole lot better than saying barren, although she wasn't barren. No, whenever she thinks of herself back then it's almost always spring, or summer. It's as if the fruit's always just about to, Lori thinks, and she sees the valley in its deep greens, she sees a bowl of cherries on the table.

Children next door, she thinks, two little toddlers, and of course it's all dried up in there now, there's nothing to be done with a network of cast iron pipes like hers and she thinks, it was a Saturday afternoon, the day they moved in, a Saturday afternoon in early spring and the sun was swinging in and out of tall clouds, and yes, she remembers carrying their things across the yard and into their little house. Joe's records and books, a bag of clothes each.

And Lori steps out of the kitchen door into the yard. That's us just about moved in, she thinks, and she looks across the valley at the fell, and well, it hardly seems possible that she should be here, that Joseph from the School of Music should want to, no, but here they are, she thinks, here we are, and she stands in the yard and looks over at the fell, and she can say with some certainty that she hasn't ever stood so close to something so, and Lori thinks, imposing. Even the Post Office Tower in Lionel Street doesn't make her feel as small as she feels now. Although it sways when the wind's up, she thinks. She won't walk under it. She said as much to Joe the other week and he said, my Lo.

He calls her his Lo, yes, my Lo, he says whenever he feels like saying, and she thinks, like a butterfly, a small skipper in long grass. He's in the ends of her fingers, in her scalp, her ears.

And Lori looks along the line of fells running north. Each one a catastrophe of sorts, she thinks, yes, each one a memory of the earth shifting. Shuddering, she thinks, and she thinks, my Lo, my Lo, and she takes a few steps towards the little fence that separates their yard and the next-door yard and she sees that in the far corner of the next-door yard there are two small boys kneeling on the ground opposite each other, a boy wearing a red coat and a boy wearing a green coat, and she sees that the boy in red is pushing a toy tractor. He pushes the tractor in a circle around his body, he pushes it around his knees and then around his back and he does it again, makes a circle with the tractor, a sort of loop around his little body, and Lori stands at the fence and she hears the boy in green say, my turn, and she watches as the boy in red pushes the tractor around his back again.

Chug, chug, chug, he says, and he pushes the tractor over a lump of mud, he pushes it slowly, he pushes it in a wide arc around his knees and his back and the boy in green stands up and says, it's not fair, but the boy in red goes on pushing, slowly he pushes. Chug, chug, chug, he says, and Lori thinks, come on, give the other boy a turn and she looks around the yard and she sees clothes hanging on next-door's line, she sees two pairs of little brown trousers, a blue jumper, a grey jumper and she thinks,

the trousers and the jumpers must belong to the boys, and
Lori turns and sees that, yes, there's already a line here for
them, for her and Joseph and she hears the boy in green say,
Emile, Emile, and she watches Emile push the tractor
around his body and she thinks that sooner or later things
will be the same for Joe and her, it'll be tractors in the yard,
she thinks, it'll be a lot more washing and hanging things
out, and she thinks, why not? if they've come as far as
they've come. Everyone starts somewhere, everyone begins
with records and books and a bagful of clothes. It's the way
people begin. And where's Joseph now, Lori thinks, because
she wants to tell him there are two small boys living next
door, that the boys are out in the yard right this moment
if he wants to come and see, and she thinks, brown hair, not
black, and she hears the boy in green say, Emile, my turn
Emile, and she hears Emile say, no, not yet, no, and Lori
turns and walks towards the house, she looks in through
the living room window and she thinks, well of course,
because inside she sees Joseph kneeling on the floor with
his records around him, one hundred records, Lori thinks,
at least, and she watches as he picks up a record and puts
it down again and she thinks, his first love, yes, she'd have
to be blind not to notice the way he touches the records.
With his beautiful hands, his beautiful fingers. And she
knows nothing about music herself, no, she doesn't understand the first thing and Lori stands there outside the
living room window and she feels a cold wind come across
the yard and she thinks, despite the sun, yes, the sun is so,
and she thinks, detached, and she looks in through the
window and she sees Joseph pull a record from its sleeve
and put it on the turntable, she sees the arm come across
and she hears the boy in green say, Emile, Emile, mum said,

and the music starts playing and Lori thinks, strings, yes, he's taught her that much, and the sound of the strings comes out through the window and she turns and looks across the valley at the fell, and well, she can hardly tell which is bigger, the fell or the music, and she hears the music come out and she thinks, it's as if someone's pulling it, yes, one long thread of music, and she stands in the yard, she stands outside the living room window and the music comes out in a long thread and she thinks, the music will just keep coming and coming, yes, the record will keep, she thinks, and she hears one of the boys saying, chug, chug, chug. The boy in green at last, yes, the boy in green has finally got his turn, and she doesn't know which is bigger, the fell or the music or the small boys next door, and she feels the cold come across the yard and she thinks, all these huge things, yes, all at once, and she watches as Joseph opens up the little window and calls through the gap.

Bartók or Ravel? what's your guess then Lo, Bartók or Ravel? and Lori doesn't know one from the other, she doesn't know the first thing about classical music.

Guess? she says, I can't guess, how am I supposed to guess? and she hears the strings moving in and out of each other, passing over and under each other like snakes, Lori thinks, or lovers, and Joseph says, just guess, and he looks so happy, this brown-haired boy of hers, he looks so, Lori thinks.

Beautiful fingers, long, long fingers, and she says, Ravel? No, Bartók? and she says, no Joseph, it isn't fair, and Joseph laughs and he shakes his head, and she sees his long hair shaking around his neck and his shoulders.

Shame on you Lo, it's Ravel, it's old Maurice, and she hears the *r* come from the back of his throat. It makes him almost a stranger, she thinks, and she watches as he shuts the little window and kneels down by the record player and Lori thinks, look at him, it's as if he's hardly, she thinks, it's as if the music.

And she doesn't know what she means, no, she gets distracted by him, by his hair, by his beautiful hands and she thinks, play your music then, yes, play on. And she looks out at the fell and she looks over at the two boys in the next-door yard and she thinks, go on inside now, go and sit with Joe and his music for a while and she feels the cold come across in a single slice.

I'm coming in, she says, and she taps on the living room window and she thinks, a little washing line, already in place.

We listened to the whole quartet that afternoon, Lori thinks, then the first eight bars of the second movement, of *Assez vif, très rythmé*, over and over, until he was sure she could hear where the accents fell, and well, now she knows. The body doesn't forget, she thinks, even if it was 1974, and she thinks, nineteen seventy-four, which feels like yesterday, although she isn't sure about yesterday. He's the one who does the bins, she thinks, she can't be expected, and she thinks, the 25th or the 26th of November? And she thinks, *Assez vif, très rythmé* on the day we moved in, which by all accounts was an auspicious start because if it had been up to her it would have been 'Scarborough Fair'. And well, she has to say that he's taught her something about the world. She wouldn't have bothered with Ravel or Bartók or any of the others if it wasn't for Joseph, yes, music's important, she thinks, and it was Saturday afternoon, they still had Sunday, and after they'd listened they went out into the yard. They stood and watched as cloud shadows slid down the fellside and across the valley floor. We didn't have anything but records and clothes and books, Lori thinks, and the view across the valley, which still seems like new and she thinks, we stood and watched until he took the top of my arm with his beautiful hands and turned me towards the low fence.

And Lori sees a man and a woman standing there on the other side of the fence.

Welcome to the village, the woman says, and Lori sees the woman's hands resting there on her swollen belly.

Welcome to Troutbeck, the woman says, and Lori looks at the woman's belly and thinks, no time wasted there, two boys in the yard and already and the woman says, welcome, welcome to Troutbeck and she sweeps her arm the length of the valley.

Thank you, yes, Lori says, and she looks along the valley, she looks along the line of fells and she sees snow resting in the gullies and she thinks, down here it's just about spring, yes, look at Joseph with his toes coming out of his sandals when there's snow up there on top and Lori thinks, he runs warm and she hears the woman say, not long to go with this one, this one here.

No, yes, says Lori, and you've already got boys, two boys?

Twins, the woman says, Felix and Emile, and she looks over at the two boys in the far corner of the yard. Felix, Emile, she says, boys, she says, but the boys don't turn and the woman says, boys, come on, and the man says, leave them, and he passes a box of eggs over the fence to Joseph.

Eggs, fantastic, thank you, Joseph says.

Laid this morning, fresh, the man says, and Lori looks

at the small boys playing over in the far corner of the yard. Playing with a stick, she thinks, or perhaps a little spade, and well, she can't quite see, no.

Paul and Annie, the man says.

Joseph and Lori, Joseph says, Joe and Lo, if you like.

And Paul calls to the two boys, yes, he wants them to come over now, he wants them to come and say their hellos.

Boys, boys, he says, and the boys turn and look.

Felix, Emile, Paul says, and the boy in the green coat gets up and runs over to the woodpile.

Felix, Annie says, over here. And the boy stands by the woodpile. Felix, Annie says, come on, she says.

And Lori feels the cold come across the yard and she slips her arm around Joseph's waist and she thinks, what's this, because Felix pulls something off the woodpile, yes, the thing flops down from the woodpile, and oh, Lori thinks, it's a cat, yes, and the little boy walks towards the low fence with his arms wrapped around the ginger cat's chest. The boy is so small that the cat's legs are almost dragging.

Here, he says as he walks. Here. Here. And the cat's paws scuff the ground, but the boy leans back. Here, Felix says. Here's Marsalis.

And Lori looks down at the sodden earth. She remembers so much, she thinks, even up here in the fog she doesn't have any trouble remembering. The images and words arrive by themselves. It isn't as if she has to conjure them up, no, they just come, the same words and images from all those years ago.

It was only a week later that the first real sun of the year arrived, yes, that was the first one, Lori thinks. She remembers pulling open the curtains. It was almost completely dark out there, she thinks, yes, the light was just at the point of arriving. They'd only been there a week, seven days, hardly any time at all, and she went downstairs and opened the back door, she stepped down into the yard and looked out over the valley.

Day really is only just coming on, Lori thinks, yes, the light is just at the point of breaking through, and well, she feels sure it's here already, the first real sun of the year, and she stands in the yard in her pyjamas, she stands there looking out over the valley at the fell and she feels the cold coming up through her feet and she thinks, let it come up, because soon the sun will arrive, yes, the first real sun of the year, and she looks right out, she stares right out and she feels the horizon falling away, she feels the earth slowly turning, and well, it really does come from nothing, Lori thinks, the start of day, yes, it's almost a miracle that darkness should be replaced by light, that the earth should go on turning. And it's been a good few days, yes, now they're settled things will happen. The wheels are set in motion, she thinks, for tractors, for trucks in the yard, for tiny clothes on the line, a little red jumper, a pair of brown trousers, Lori thinks, and she understands these things take time but she's looking out across the valley and she sees that the light is slowly coming on, that the fell is starting to colour, and well, yes, she feels certain these things will happen. It's a small feeling, she says to herself, but still, standing here in their little yard she has the sensation that the earth is slowly turning towards the east, that things are more or less predictable, that even the first real sun of the year is more or less predictable, and Lori takes a couple of steps back towards the house. She'll make coffee now. She'll wake Joseph and tell him the first real sun is on its way, and she stands there by the door and she knows that sooner or later the boys will come out into the yard, already she knows this, that the boys will come out to play, yes, she's fallen right into the pattern of things, and she thinks, Felix and Emile, well, she wouldn't have expected names like that, not in this place of crags and brows and folds, and she'll go inside and start on the coffee, yes, get it brewing at least, she thinks, and Lori takes another step towards the back door. She's got time, she thinks, before the sun comes up over the fell, yes, she's got a bit of time, although she can feel it, the earth, slowly turning eastwards and well, no, she won't go back inside just yet, she'll stay here in the yard and watch the sun come up from behind the fell, yes, this is what she really wants to do, she thinks, and she lifts her arms, she spreads her arms and she sees that her arms hold so much more than this one fell, that, yes, she's cradling the whole line of fells, from south to north, as far as Thornthwaite Crag, and further, she thinks, and she stretches and stretches and she sees that the darkness has almost left, she sees the fell fall inside another light and she understands how restless it is, yes, this feeling, something tightening then slackening, a huge thing, Lori thinks. And she must be half asleep still, to be going on like this out here in the yard, yes, it's almost ridiculous to think she feels the earth slowly turning, and she'll go on inside and make coffee, she'll leave the back door open, she thinks, yes, why not, because in all truth she isn't ready to go inside, no, she can't go inside yet, and Lori looks out across the valley at the fell and she thinks, Big Ranulph, and she feels his absence push up against her temples and she thinks, so many things get caught inside, and well, coffee will help, if anything's going to take her mind off missing Big Ranulph it'll be a good cup of coffee and she turns and sees in next-door's yard three, no, two dead chickens. Two dead chickens and three heads, and Lori stands by the back door and tries to match the heads to the chickens. Stop matching, she thinks, there isn't any point in matching, and she thinks, how has she missed the feathers, when the feathers are everywhere? brown feathers, white, a kind of deep red, feathers in a pile by the laurel bush and on both sides of the low fence. They've only lived here a week, she thinks, seven days, hardly any time at all and this morning she woke to the first real sun, yes, she's sure it's coming, the first real sun of the year, and now brown feathers, white, a kind of deep red, and Lori sees Annie step out of the back door into the next-door yard, yes, there's Annie, standing outside her back door wearing nothing but her nightdress. How about that? Lori thinks, the pair of them out here in their nightwear, yes, here they are in their yards, Lori in her pyjamas, Annie in her nightie with her belly full of baby and Lori watches as Annie takes a step forwards, her hands on her hips, her fingers pressing into her back, and Lori looks down at the feathers and she looks over at Annie and the pair of them are standing outside their back doors, the cold is coming up from the ground, Lori thinks, and well, she can't go inside for socks now, no, it's too late for socks because all these feathers have settled in the yard, soft feathers, Lori thinks, and she looks over at Annie again and she sees that her weight is all wrong, there's too much out front and she thinks, the baby will have to come soon, yes, she can see for herself that there can't be many days left before the baby arrives, and they're so young, Annie and Lori, yes, the pair of them have hardly started on life and now there are these feathers, these chicken heads and bodies.

Sooner or later the sun will come up over the fell, Lori thinks, the first real sun of the year, yes, she felt it the moment she opened her eyes this morning and she thinks, the sun is so predictable, and she watches as Annie makes her way over to the low fence.

The fox? Lori says.

Yes, says Annie. They never take more than one, kill as many as they can get their jaws on.

Yes, says Lori, although she knows nothing about foxes, no, how can she know about foxes when they've only lived here a week, seven days, hardly any days at all, and Annie says, only three heads, she'll bet on the others hiding somewhere. In the laurel perhaps, she says, up in the cherry tree. They'll fly if the fox has given them enough of a fright, and Lori says, yes, yes, and she thinks, so many things she doesn't know still, no, she hardly knows anything and she watches as Annie squats down to pick up a head. One of the Leghorns, Annie says, and Lori looks at the white head and she looks at Annie squatting down there in the yard with the feathers, with the swell of belly between her knees and she thinks, in all its preciousness, in all its, and she wants to say beauty, yes, that's what she wants to say, and she thinks, it won't be long, no, sooner or later the first real sun of the year will lie across the valley floor but now she needs to help Annie with these feathers, with these bodies and heads, and all of a sudden Lori feels so young, so young and so old at the same time, yes, only a few years ago she was a girl and now there are these feathers, Lori thinks, these bodies and heads, and the baby will come soon, another baby already, and then there's Joseph, she thinks, sleeping upstairs in their little house, and she looks out across the valley and she feels so old, all these things, the wrong things, piling up inside her and she thinks, help with the feathers at least, if you can't manage a whole bird, and she steps over the little fence and she hears Annie say, thanks, yes, come on over, and Lori looks down at the heads and the bodies and she says, the home stretch for you then, Annie? And Annie stands up, she stands in the yard holding the chicken head and Lori sees that things can't go on the way they are for Annie, no, the baby will soon be in the world, and she bends down to pick up a head and she sees, yes, four or five pink flowers there on the cherry tree. A spring baby, that's what we're in for, Lori thinks, and she picks up the heads and carries them over to the woodpile. Yes, here by the woodpile for the heads, she thinks, and she goes and gets the chickens, the white chicken, the deep red chicken. Everything by the woodpile, out of harm's way, and now she'll go on in and fetch the broom. No, Annie says, no, she shouldn't sweep, not without shoes, she'll already have waded through enough chicken mess and Lori looks at the soles of her feet and she says, they'll wash, and she stands there facing their little house and she thinks, twenty-eight years old, and she says, if you need anything else.

No, Annie says, she'll get Paul on to the sweeping, give him a job to do, yes, they do better with a job, with something in their hands.

Lori's inside making coffee. The boys are already out in the yard, yes, there they are, Felix and Emile, trapping feathers under their wellies, brown feathers, white feathers, and she carried the deep red chicken across the yard, it hardly felt like an animal, a bird, Lori thinks, it was as if the deep red chicken had finally relaxed. And she'll take the coffee upstairs, she'll open up the windows and let the fresh air in because it won't be long until the sun comes around, yes, the first real sun of the year, and Lori thinks, white feathers and brown feathers, deep red, and now she sees that the other chickens have come back. Three chickens there at the feeder, yes, going along as usual, and she gets a couple of mugs from the cupboard, the olive mugs, she thinks, and she pours the coffee out.

That spring baby was Ross, Lori thinks. The day he was born the wind eddied the cherry blossom around the yards. It was a hard spring, she thinks, we lost the whole of April to rain. And Lori looks down at the sodden earth beneath her boots and she thinks, yes, she's used to it, to damp socks and sleeves, to damp walls and floors, she's used to the groundwater rising and everything she touches, yes, even the sheets, she thinks, although they can't be, no, the sheets are dry, she thinks, as long as the bed's kept away from the wall and she thinks, there wasn't a fine day until the second week in May, yes, she'd almost stopped believing and then, and Lori thinks, Felix, Emile and baby Ross. And that was just the start, just the beginning of a long line of children and the catch in her throat, which was to be expected, Joe said, in a house that keeps the water in as well as it keeps it out. And she could have coped with three, with Felix, Emile and Ross, and a catch in the throat, she thinks, which was more like a narrowing than a catch. A constriction of sorts, Lori thinks. They'd only lived there a month, hardly any time at all, and if she'd just waited a bit before opening her big mouth things might have happened between her and Joe, yes, things might have worked out for the best if she'd just held on without saying, and how about it? Because what kind of question is that anyway? Lori thinks, what kind of person says to a man they hardly know, how about it, a family of our own? And she can feel the question even now, yes, the stomach for stupidity too, she thinks, and he pressed his fork so far into his mash the prongs disappeared, God, yes, the mash slipped over his fork like molten lava. Too much milk, she thinks, yes, too liberal with the milk as usual and she looks down at her boots and she thinks, my God, because she isn't exactly striding, no, she can hardly get her feet above the rough, and well, that had gone and ruined dinner, hadn't it? Mash, when she could have settled on new potatoes, yes, she'd almost done a panful of baby potatoes, butter, salt, parsley, and how about it? How about it? she'd said, and what was the poor man supposed to say to that, Lori thinks.

He's dead. He's dead up there on our bed, Lori thinks, and
she waits to see if she feels anything, something, and well,
she doesn't. You can't go forcing a thing if it won't come
on its own, she thinks, and Lori looks down at her boots.
She's too late with the leather, she thinks, and she thinks
of those photos you get, the ones of huge river deltas and
she thinks of the boy who put his finger in the dike and she
thinks, what's that got to do with anything? And she'll hunt
out the neatsfoot anyway and she thinks, Moor Head, yes,
then she'll decide, and she feels the cold around her middle,
or perhaps around her heart, although she's never been
able to pinpoint where the heart is exactly, and she thinks
of all those diagrams you get, the ones of lungs and kidneys
and intestines and she thinks, slippery yellows and pinks
and browns and reds, and she's supposed to feel something,
if all those obituaries she reads are true, if the time she
spends in the back pages of *The Gazette* is worth anything
at all, and Lori thinks, Joseph and Lori Fitzgerald are
delighted to announce, no, Joe and Lori proudly announce,
and she thinks, the safe arrival of their much awaited, and
she thinks, daughter or son? and she looks down at her
boots and she thinks, not this, Lori, we're past all this, and
she sees her boots moving over the rough ground, grasses
and sedges, swollen mosses and it's with great sadness that
we announce the passing.

Empty, she thinks, apart from the stomach, although
the stomach's for disappointment, she's almost sure, yes,
the eyes for sadness, the stomach for disappointment.
But no, she thinks, it's as if the whole damn thing sits down
there in her bowels and never shifts, and she thinks of

those diagrams you get and she thinks, there's something
repulsive, and the hand will slip inside her jacket if she
wants it to, if she can keep the fucker still, she thinks, and
she can't, no, she can't, and in all truth she's stopped wanting it, although the emptiness weighs and she thinks, sticks
and stones and she thinks of Annie with her swollen bellies,
six swollen bellies, all that life she pushed out into the
world, yes, miracle after tiny miracle and Lori feels it right
down there in her bowels and she thinks, if it's anything
at all it's resentment, yes, or something pushing, because it
isn't exactly a giant leap to say pushing, if that's what she
really feels, and she thinks, no. No, no, she's finished with
wanting. All she's got left is some kind of, and she thinks,
sediment. And she sees her future there in front of her,
a dark blue-grey, and she looks at her boots and she thinks
of those aerial photographs you get and she thinks, there's
something repulsive

    a sedentary body of water

    silt, sand and gravel

and she can't ignore it, this pushing, and she thinks, not
pushing, no, more like pressing, because there now,
yes, now she feels it, something pressing, something almost
grinding down there. The baby's ready to come out after
all, Lori thinks, yes, sticks and stones, and she thinks,
big broken bones, and she feels a pressure, she feels a
heaviness. At last, she thinks, and she lets the fog slip in,
slip out, and she thinks, in and out, in and out with the
fog, and she pushes her boots over the rough ground
and she feels a flush of warmth down there, yes, she feels
the warmth rushing and she thinks, it's like those aerial
photographs you get. The river finally spreads, and she's
so cold, she's, and she pats herself down there, she gives

herself a few small pats around and she can't tell, no, she's never been able to, and well, no, it's really, she thinks, yes, broken waters. And she's almost at Moor Head, too far from anywhere, and she thinks of the woman who gave birth outside Morgan Dental. Little baby Florence, Lori thinks, and of course Joe was right, they should have stopped with *The Gazette*.

If all it does is make you upset, love.

And Lori looks into the fog and she thinks, we'll just have to get ourselves comfortable over by the wall there, and she feels her belly tighten into stone and she thinks, mudstone, siltstone, and she thinks, a little head, yes, of all the things she could be carrying, a head, and sticks and stones and she says, congratulations, yes, congratulations again, and she walks towards the wall and she thinks, down here will be fine, and she looks at the place where her belly should be

and she thinks, dear God.

The peat, the grasses. All the mosses look so similar, so wet, and she says, congratulations, and she thinks.

Up onto Sallows then home on the Garburn, she thinks, and she pats around herself, she pats down there and she thinks, just walk now, because she can't be more than a kilometre from the top of Sallows, and she thinks, you've come this far. You don't walk all the way to Moor Head only to end up following the wall on down to the Nook.

And isn't she the same as Joe? Aren't we the same, she thinks? Me with my knotts and pikes and scars and brows, him with his arias and cantatas and whatever else. Tops and crags and heads and gills, she thinks, sides and passes and stones, and she thinks, it's all music, no, it all sings is what she really means, and Lori feels her trousers sticking and she pats around, she pats down there and she thinks, it all sings.

Felix, Emile, Ross, Charlotte, Louise, Silas.

Yes, she still says Felix, Emile, Ross, Charlotte, Louise, Silas, when everyone else in the village has forgotten about them, or almost forgotten, Lori thinks, and she can say with her hand on her heart that she's never laid a finger on anybody in her whole life, no, the only things she's ever laid are eyes, and she thinks, feel that now? yes, the pelvis is lighter. Although it's the space that weighs on you, yes, all those years of dropping fat and muscle when it's the emptiness that won't shift.

The house knows, she thinks. Every time she drags herself across the bedroom floor there's a juddering. Walls and boards, she thinks, a kind of repulsion, yes, the house hates her! It started when she spilt the sugar and couldn't bring herself to finish sweeping, she thinks, and she won't deny it, the feeling's mutual, the feeling of repulsion, she means. The flagstones secrete a kind of sticky mucus. And what does Joe think to that?

It's nothing but slugs, love. Huge gastropods, he says, mmm.

We're not beyond a joke, Lori thinks, no, we like to, she thinks, and she pushes on over the sodden earth, one foot in front of the other and if it wasn't for the fog she'd turn and look back at the mound of grass the way she always does. It's nice to see where you've been, she thinks, and she feels the scones there in her pocket and she thinks, she may as well, yes, she must need some food inside her by now, and she almost left the house empty-handed this morning, yes, she was halfway out of the front door when she remembered, and well, she wouldn't usually walk across the kitchen floor in boots, no, she'd rather go through the whole rigmarole of getting the boots off and on again than face the prospect of sweeping. Anything but sweeping, Lori thinks, and the boots were clean enough. She got two scones from the tin on the side and put them in her jacket pocket, and she only has to think about the broom, she only has to think about things that move like that, although a broom doesn't move like anything, and she thinks, get the scones down you, raisins and all, and she pushes her boots over the sodden earth, yes, walk fifty miles, walk one hundred miles, she thinks, and it seems like forever since he said, yes, the way he always says,

You on for the *Nine O'Clock*, love?

And she thinks, when hasn't she? been on for the *Nine O'Clock*, she means, because out of the two of them, she's the one who actually shows some interest. The moment the headlines are through he pushes down on the arm of the sofa. She hears its little wooden feet knocking, she hears her vertebrae. Like Lego, she thinks, and he works his feet into his slippers, he stands himself up.

If that's all they've got for us tonight, he says.

And she lines up her incisors and counts, or she doesn't count. Either way her jaw's so used to twitching it does it involuntarily. How many times a day, she thinks, slippers across the flagstones, a drag harrow over sticky soil, and she doesn't know what it is about the kitchen, the way it handles noise, she means. It can't absorb. A mat would help, yes, a mat would make all the difference in there, Lori thinks. They should go on into town and find something, she couldn't care one way or the other about colour as long as it isn't too bright, she thinks. You can't have too much of a thing in a small house like ours, and one thing's for sure, she'll never get used to the bedroom carpet as long as she lives. Pink, she thinks, and she doesn't know why they don't, she doesn't know why they haven't, and she thinks, forget it, all she can do is pull the door shut every time she passes. Or don't pass, she thinks, yes, she's always saying don't pass, because she's finished with trying to get the door to shut after a big rain, yes, she's done with all its expanding and contracting, and she needs to eat, although the scones are old, yes, it happened overnight, the scones getting old, going a little bit stale, and she walked across the flagstones in her boots this morning, she took one scone, then another from the tin on the side. Eat the lump and leave the crumbs, she thinks, yes, the lump's probably the fresh bit, and her hands are so cold, her fingers are white, a ghosty type of white, Lori thinks, and she could die up here, perish, she means, although she's never heard of it, a small fell like this. It's always Helvellyn, Blencathra, Scafell Pike, it's always a crag or an edge that takes someone.

Tourists normally, Lori thinks, yes, the fells don't hesitate if they sense a weakness, and everything Joe says about tourists he gets from old John and Lizzie, and well, she isn't surprised they've got something to say about tourists over there, three lambs mauled by dogs in the space of two months, Lori thinks, last spring, yes, she remembers old Lizzie saying,

One of them a labradoodle too, would you have it?

And Lori thinks, what's a? and no, she couldn't care, and she's seen the tourists parking their cars in front of gates, she's seen them skirting the edge of Top Field, looking for a place to climb over.

Private land means nothing to them, love.

The workings of too much money is what you're witnessing, yes, that's what Joe likes to say, although he gets it from, well, yes, she knows where he gets it and she thinks, who's that then? because, yes, she can hear something, she can hear someone and she looks around and there isn't anyone and she thinks, the worst we ever get with tourists is a dropped wrapper or two out on the lane, which hardly matters when Janet goes out picking on a Saturday morning anyway, Janet and one or two others from Town End way, she thinks, and who in God's name is up here on a day like today? and she thinks, whoever it is can just sod off. She's too tired, yes, and now her trousers, this wet, she thinks, and she pats down there, she pats around and she thinks, you can't tell, no, you can't see, and she pushes her feet across the rough ground and she hears people talking, and no, she thinks, she can't face anything right now, and she pats around and she thinks, stop patting, because every time she does there's a smell, and now there's someone, probably two people up here, yes, and she thinks, you can sit down and wait for them to pass, you can come off the path here, and she comes off the path and she thinks, keep coming then, and she takes a few more steps and she thinks, come on, yes, have a little sit down, God knows she could do with one, and if she really wants to go to the top there's time, and she looks around her and she thinks, it could be late already, or early still, yes, it's probably not much later than, and she thinks, sit down, sit yourself. And she started out so early. It was only just getting light, yes, the light was just coming through the darkness.

How slow she's got, yes, she's almost got to the point, she thinks.

And she thinks, twenty-five, of course, if they've lived
here twenty-five years, and she waited sixteen long months
after he was born before asking Joe again about starting a
family, and she thinks, we'd got to know each other by then,
yes, one winter up here was enough to knock the corners
off, and she thinks of the way it rains down south and she
thinks, even when it's heavy it's not, no, it isn't anything
like, and when the water came up through the floor and
made a pool in the porch he stuck his finger in.

Well, Lo, we're not exactly going to be drowning in it.

And then he went along to the Post Office for coffee.
Ten minutes later he arrived home with a jar of Nescafé,
Nescafé, and a lump in his throat. The coffee was shit,
his job was shit and his socks were wet, and not only his
socks, he said, not only his.

And to think I've got a degree from the School of Music.

Or perhaps it was the Royal School of Music, Lori
thinks, and she takes a few steps off the path and she
thinks, she waited through all that, she waited until their
second summer before asking him again, and she stands
in the fog and she thinks of Felix and Emile out there in
the yard and she thinks, one long day pressed against the
next without ever really, and she takes a few more steps off
the path and she stands in the grasses, in the peat water
and she pictures herself at the window, she pictures herself
wearing the apron with the thick navy and white stripes.

And Lori looks up at the clock on the wall and she thinks,
almost nine, yes, she'll have to start thinking about shutting

the place up for the night, and she turns and looks back into the yard and she sees the boys are still there, are going on with their game and she thinks, how many hours of filling and pouring? And she watches as Emile puts the watering can under the garden tap, she watches as the water hits the plastic, as the water sprays and falls, and she thinks, look how wet their shorts are, their legs. Emile's T-shirt too, she thinks, because every time he turns the tap it all runs down, and she thinks, it's almost nine. And still the light. And she hears the swifts somewhere over by the farm and she thinks, everyone's playing out late, yes, they're all, and she looks out onto the lane and she sees that the daisies are wide open, are turned towards the setting sun. These twilights they're getting now, Lori thinks, these twilights that never pitch into night, and she pulls the apron over her head and hangs it on its little hook, and she hears Annie calling.

Felix, Emile, boys.

She hears the water coming out from the tap and she thinks she'll not shut the back door tonight, no, and she hears Annie calling.

They were out there every day, from first thing until late, Lori thinks, although she can't say when it started, with the watching, she means, and if anything you just come on to a thing, yes, that's how it was, she'd have her tea at the window after work and later she'd come out into the yard awhile, yes, wasn't that the year she started with the patch, with runner beans and courgettes? And something else, Lori thinks, and she thinks, most likely radishes, and well, she wasn't up for growing much else, no, she never really did much good out in the patch, and Lori looks at her boots

down there in the peat water. She remembers how much
dust there was that year, yes, even the drought of '76 didn't
bring as much as we had then, and she thinks, grit really,
not dust, and she only has to remember and she's got it
between her teeth again, yes, how many times a day did she
brush and swill, and still? She'd stand and watch the chickens sift it through their feathers, she'd watch them kick
it up. It came down on both sides of the fence, Lori thinks,
and settled in a thin film, yes, dust on the laurel, dust on
the car and under her nails. Grit really, and he'd ask her if
she was washing the veg before boiling it and Lori stands a
few steps off the path and she thinks, wash the veg yourself,
wash it your-bloody.

They stayed out until nine, sometimes later, Lori thinks.
She got used to watching the window of light above the fell,
she got used to waiting for Annie to stand at the back door.
Felix, Emile, boys, Lori thinks, and there weren't enough
hours until morning. That's how it felt, as if there weren't
enough hours until they started again, although every
morning it happened, Felix and Emile, under a clean sun.
Trucks and sticks and water and stones, Lori thinks, and
there wasn't any end to it, no, she couldn't see any.
    And Lori goes to rub her eyes, although the eyes are
fine, yes, the eyes are just another way of seizing her
attention and she thinks, Ross, yes, Ross too and walking
already, between the woodpile and the laurel, between the
laurel and the washing line. Little T-shirts, little trousers,
little shorts, Lori thinks, red, blue, brown, yellow, and the
feeling when Annie took them down. The same emptiness,
Lori thinks.

IT WAS LATE THAT SUMMER WHEN SHE FINALLY SAID SOMETHING

It was the day Annie came knocking on the window asking for brown sugar, the day the smell of cut grass had turned the air sweet. It was two hundred grams she wanted, Lori thinks, or perhaps it was two-hundred and fifty.

If you've got some to spare, Annie says, if you wouldn't mind, and she stands at the open window with her hands on her hips, with a little flush in her face, and Lori says, plenty of sugar here, Joe likes to keep a spare one in, and she takes a couple of steps towards the cupboard and she hears Annie say, so we've got a bit of news over our way. And Lori turns and walks back over to the open window.

Another baby! Annie says.

And Lori puts her hands in her apron pockets and she thinks, smile at least, at least manage.

All things told it was a bit of a shock, not exactly part of the plan, Annie says, and she knows she shouldn't say that, but here they are, here we are, and Lori pulls her hands out from her apron pocket and she says, congratulations, congratulations anyway, shock or no shock, and already she feels it down there in her stomach, like oats, Lori thinks, and she says, was it two hundred or two-fifty you were after with the sugar? And Annie says, two hundred if you wouldn't mind, and Lori takes a couple of steps towards the cupboard and she hears Annie say, thank God for you, Lo, because the last thing she feels like doing is dragging the boys down to the Post Office for sugar when all she'll get in return for her efforts is a fight, over chocolate footballs of all things. No one with kids of their own would even think about putting the jar up on the counter the way she has it in there. Asking for trouble, Annie says, and Lori thinks, she's never noticed, all those times in there and she's never even.

And if it's been a month it's been a year, Annie says, since she's left the house without one or other or all of the boys in tow, and she'd give her right arm, or her left one, come to think of it, just to shut the door and leave it all behind for an hour or two, and Lori says, yes, well, if you ever need me to.

And if she could just do her business on the toilet, if she could get that simple business done without being interrupted, and Lori looks through the open window and she thinks, there's a freshness about Annie's face, there's something, and she wants to say vital, and she feels the breeze come in through the open window, she feels it step and settle and she says, yes, yes and she sees the way Annie's face moves, the way her body moves, and she thinks.

Although this one feels different somehow, Annie says, all fingers crossed for a girl, although no, she doesn't really mean, they don't mean, no, give them a happy, healthy baby and they'll be happy too, but it's one thing after another with the boys at the moment, and Lori must have seen the way they traipse in and out of the house, she must see all that from over here, and it's more than she can manage to get them to take their wellies off, she's given up on it, you give up on it.

And Lori says, I'll get the sugar now.

Two hundred grams if you don't mind, Annie says, two hundred should be enough to sweeten these early apples we've got coming. They'll only go to waste if I don't put them in a pie, and she says, there isn't a breath today, is there? and she looks across the valley at the fell and she pushes her hair behind her ear and says, no, not a breath.

Yes, she'd passed the sugar through the window and later that day, whilst she was clearing away the dinner, she'd said, did you know they're having another baby next door? She was wearing her summer dress, and Lori thinks, a summer dress and she hears a voice somewhere in the fog and she thinks, dear God, because she'd as good as forgotten she was up here in the fog and she thinks, it was late, yes, too late in the year for a summer dress and she feels how wet she is down there and she thinks, don't pat, and she takes a couple of stiff steps, her hips, she thinks, or her groin, and she sees a young man and a young woman walking towards her and she thinks, walkers, yes, it's in the gait, and she thinks, who else but walkers? And she hears Joe saying, a right to roam, a right to ruddy well roam and she thinks, we're not beyond a joke, no, we've never gone so far that, and if she isn't mistaken the fog's lifting, or shifting, and she thinks, Berghaus jackets, red, blue, and she thinks, fuck off, won't you? Berkshire, Hertfordshire, she thinks, the ruddy Home Counties, and they haven't been further south than Wigan for a decade. Longer, Lori thinks, and now the man is saying something, yes, she can see the man is talking, she can see his mouth moving, his head too, bobbing a little bit and she thinks, where is she? because she can't hear a thing he's saying and she thinks, walk one hundred miles, Lori, and the man and the woman are standing right next to her, she watched them walk over just a moment ago, yes, she saw the pair of them striding over in their red and blue Berghaus jackets, and she thinks, where has this dog come from then? because there's a black dog leaning against the woman's leg and she thinks, perhaps the fog isn't lifting after all, if a dog can appear just like that.

And the summer dress was OK, it was fine, and she thinks, don't cry now, no, she's had the whole day for crying and she's wasted it, and Lori brings her jaw forward so her teeth line up and she doesn't even like scones. She hates them. He gets a bag of four or six every time he goes to town. She's always having to eat her way through them. There must've been hundreds, Lori thinks, hundreds and hundreds of scones brought up from town and every time she opens the tin she thinks, no, not more scones, and she thinks, don't cry, and she sees that the man and the woman and the dog are still standing there next to her and well, she could easily slip what's left of the scones to the dog, and Lori puts her hand in her pocket and she thinks, she can't give crumbs to the dog, no, she can't go sprinkling crumbs for a big dog like that. Let the crows have them then. There'll be enough crows on the fellside until dusk, past dusk and she stands there on the open fell and she thinks, there isn't anything better than watching a pair of crows head home. Of all things, she thinks, and she thinks, a crow's wings beat so deeply, yes, a crow really flies and the man and the woman and the dog are standing right next to her and she thinks, who comes up here in fog like this? and she sees the man's head bobbing a little bit, she sees the fog settled wet on his hair, on his face and she thinks, crow shows purple under the right sun, or green, and she thinks, don't cry, because the man is talking, the man is saying, is there anything we can do? and Lori thinks, walk fifty miles, walk one hundred and even though it was the end of summer the day was so warm, yes, she wanted to wear the summer dress, although you hardly need one in these parts, no, there are really only three or four days a year for a summer dress and she thinks, Joseph's at home on the bed

and she looks at the man's head, she looks at his glasses
moving up and down and she says, no, although her voice
comes out from somewhere else, from inside the valley
or somewhere over in the north, and she can see that the
man's straining to hear, yes, the man's leaning right in and
Lori sees her hands coming out from the sleeves of her
jacket, she sees her boots down there in the peat water
and she thinks, in summer the bogs give cottongrass and
asphodel, they give mats of pink pimpernel with flowers
so delicate they come apart the moment you touch them
and the fact that Joseph's dead is probably an emergency.
Although no, she thinks, there's never been an emergency
and she looks up and says, I'm fine. She says, I'm taking my
time, that's all, and the man and the woman say, OK, and
Lori looks at the man's glasses and she feels how wet she is
down there and she thinks now's not the time for, and the
man says, enjoy your walk, fog permitting, and Lori thinks,
if it's any voice at all it's a kind voice, and she thinks, yes,
now she feels like talking, she hasn't felt like anything all
day, not even a small piece of scone and now at last she
feels like talking and she opens her mouth and she hears
her voice come right out of it.

It looks as though the fog won't be lifting any time
soon, she says, and the woman says, no, the woman says,
it's lucky Joseph knows how to use a map and compass.

You did a winter skills training course didn't you,
darling? And Lori thinks, no, because Joseph's dead, and
she feels how wet she is down there, and cold. Cold for
hours, she thinks, and she'll say something about her
Joseph now because he's been at home all day, his eyes on
the woodchip and she thinks, it isn't a stillness, in the eyes,
she means, no, if anything the eyes are describing, and she

thinks, a lucky accident, for the eyes to fall that way, and Lori sees the man there in front of her and she thinks, another Joseph, yes, another one has appeared as if by magic. There must be hundreds of Josephs, thousands probably, all of them more or less the same, like ants, she thinks, or woodlice, because you really can't tell one woodlouse from another unless you sit them side by side, and even then you can't always, and Lori looks into the fog and she thinks, help, she thinks, please, and she sees the man and the woman and the dog walking away over the rough ground and she's sure it wasn't her who wanted the woodchip. He insisted, she thinks, and she thinks, come back. Red coat, blue coat and she can see why everyone around here hates tourists. It doesn't take much, she thinks, and she takes a few stiff steps back towards the path and she thinks, the day they moved in they lay on the living room floor and listened to Ravel.

Felix and Emile were out in the yard. Felix and Emile, Lori says, *les deux*, and she thinks, thank God, because an *x* can rest. Nothing to be done with an *x*. Although, *deux yeux*, she thinks, *Aix-en-Provence*. There's always something, and where on this earth did my Joe learn to speak French the way he does? It makes him a stranger, yes, one liaison ahead all along for him, and she puts one foot in front of the other and she thinks, that's how we'll do it, one foot then the other. One, two, she thinks, one, two, three, four and she has to say it, there isn't any getting away from it, Felix, Emile, Ross, Charlotte, Louise, Silas, she says.

Felix, Emile, Ross and another baby on the way. Pregnant again! And she shook from head to toe when she poured the sugar into a bowl for Annie that day. Two hundred grams and the rest, yes, another fifty grams at least.

She passed the bowl through the window and said, big congratulations to you then, and Annie said, yes, again, and she tapped on her belly as though it was a drum and Lori pictures herself standing there at the open window with the bowl of sugar. She sees her apron, she sees her summer dress, her yellows and pinks and reds and she thinks, too much colour, yes, she still thinks that, far too much in the way of colour and she sees herself passing the bowl of sugar through the window to Annie.

Big congratulations to you both, then, she says, and she's wearing all this colour today, she's wearing yellows and pinks and reds, she's wearing greens and oranges and she watches Annie cross the yard carrying the bowl, she watches as she goes in through her back door, as Felix then Emile then little Ross run in after her, and she sees herself in the colours and she thinks, too much of yourself, and she's standing at the kitchen window, which is where she almost always stands, and she looks down at the sugar on the floor and she feels her steadiness leaving her. The top of the head, she thinks, that's where steadiness lives, and she feels it leaving her and she thinks, get your head down, get your head between your knees and she'll end up fetching the broom, sweeping up, although the air's so heavy, the smell of cut grass, Lori thinks, since morning.

Down on the Garburn already, she thinks, and well, yes,
they were really moving, really cutting it up, and she
pushes her feet over the rough ground and down there on
the Garburn Pass she hears the man's voice, she hears its
thick spread and she thinks, jars and packets, and she
thinks of Joe pushing his slippers over the flagstones. She
juts her jaw, yes, every time she catches hold of the sound
of felt against stone she lines up her teeth. It shines a light
on them, she thinks, all the little bits she hasn't swept. And
when it comes to the sound of her own boots she's almost
comforted, yes, she likes to anticipate, and she thinks, who
doesn't? and she listens to the sound of her boots stepping,
she listens to the steady one, two. If anything can make
her settle, she thinks, and she thinks, bog moss, juniper
haircap, and beneath her stepping she hears the man down
there on the Garburn. She hears him going on and on, and
she thinks, thank God, because it's never been that way
with her and Joseph, no, neither of them ever feel the need,
and Joe's so self-contained, the only thing he ever goes on
about is the tourists, and that's OK, yes, that's fine because
he never goes too far, no, he'll have a word or two then stop,
Lori thinks. If anything she admires his self-restraint, yes,
in a world where people go on and on, Lori thinks, and
when he talks about singing he says, the sound begins in
the imagination, love, I'll say just that. And that's all he says,
Lori thinks, and she listens to her boots, to the steady one,
two and she thinks, it works for us, keeping the singing out
of the house, yes, you've got to find something that suits,
she thinks, because she worries about the roof, ever since
old John told them they'll not want to go touching the moss

up there. If you're banking on staying warm and dry.

Although that's not it, Lori thinks, that's not really it, because Joe sings like an angel. She can't put it any other way. He holds everything in that sound, she thinks, which must be more or less what an angel does and she thinks of Joe out there in the yard with his madrigals and motets and whatever else it is he likes to sing.

The truth is that it makes her uncomfortable, something so, and she thinks, heavenly, yes, a heavenly thing in this place of earth and weather, this place of mud and sediment because right from the beginning she's felt something tugging at her, pulling her down to the slaty beds. Whilst he floats, she thinks, whilst he hovers somewhere outside the white sky, and for years she's thought it. Shut up. Shut up, she thinks, when all he's doing is singing, and at some point she must have said it, get yourself on out to the yard, because for years there's been nothing more to hear in the house than the shuffling of slippers, she thinks, and she's wet, yes, she's gone and, and she thinks, no, no, and if she had half a heart she'd stand out in the yard and listen. Because how many times in a lifetime does anyone get to hear a voice like that? and she listens to her boots, their steady one, two, bog moss, she thinks, and toothed moss, although she doesn't know which and she sees Joe standing in the living room, his brown hair down around his shoulders, his mouth open as if he's doing nothing more than speaking. Always without effort for him, Lori thinks, always as if.

And Lori picks through the tub of blackberries at the kitchen table. Enough for the crumble and some to freeze, she thinks, and she turns and calls through the open door into the living room.

Apple and blackberry crumble OK for you?

You're a dream. What a dream, Lo.

And she picks through the blackberries, one, two.
Enough for a good-sized crumble, she thinks, and she
thinks, good ones in here bad ones in here, and she takes
another handful from the tub and she checks them one
by one and if they've only just gone over she'll take them,
they'll be fine once they've been cooked up, she thinks,
and she hears the tap of Joe's tuning fork, she hears it ring
and she sorts the good ones from the bad ones and after
a few long seconds he sings a note, another note and then
a scale and she picks through the blackberries, one, two,
fingers deep purple, and she thinks, not so hard with them
then, and carefully she picks and sorts. Good ones in here,
she thinks, yes, good ones here and now he's really singing,
yes, she hears it the way she hears glass, or rain, and by this
she means whatever it is that lives inside a single drop of
rain and she sorts the good ones from the bad ones and she
walks over to the kitchen door where she can see him.
Always the same, she thinks, as if her eyes are connected
to her ears and she puts her hands in her apron pocket, she
leans against the door frame and she listens to him sing,
and she thinks, thank God for singing, because he gets
himself all upset. His job, she thinks, the house, the elec-
tion, things that can't be fixed and she can't put her finger
on it, his voice, she means, yes, she's always chasing a way
to describe it and she thinks, it's enough to say beautiful,
and she looks at him standing there in their little living
room and she presses her hands deep into her apron pocket.

And Lori pushes her boots over the wet ground and she
thinks, how much further? because really she's done, yes,

really she's long past, and she thinks of all the hours of
music Joe's given her, enough music to fill the valley over
and over again, she thinks. For years it kept coming, Byrd
and Monteverdi, Ravel, she thinks, a whole collection of
strangers, their music spilling out through one of the little
top windows. And then where? Lori thinks, and she thinks,
there isn't really anything to say about the music, no, there's
only the feeling it leaves inside, yes, the music settles along
with everything else, Lori thinks, and she thinks of those
aerial photographs you get, the bars of sand and gravel
and she thinks, thank you Joe and she walks on over the
wet ground and she thinks, what on earth turns a person
as sour as she is, because she only has to see him open his
mouth out there in the yard and she thinks, what are you
doing you pillock?

Pillock, she calls him, and well, this is how things are
for her, yes, she's the one at the bottom, she's the one
slipping along on her underbelly, and when it comes to
music she doesn't know the first thing and she thinks, what
do you need to know? because if nothing else music fills
the hole inside her. Or does it open up the hole? she thinks,
and well, no, she couldn't say, although if it wasn't for Joe
she wouldn't have got herself off David Bowie or Simon and
Garfunkel. You can go round and round with 'Bridge over
Troubled Water' and it never gives you any more, she thinks,
and she supposes the record player has gone up into the
attic, yes, one of them must have, she thinks, because she
wouldn't have dared, no, nothing gets thrown out, and she
thinks, it's the TV now, it's Peter Sissons instead of Ravel,
and she thinks, more or less everyone's sucked in by the
TV and when they started out it was all records and books,
although not hers, no, she's never liked to read, it gets to

the eyes in the end, she thinks, and well, records and books are fine when you're young, when you don't have to worry about the water coming in, or the rats, and she thinks, Joseph must be young at heart to sing the way he does. He only has to flick a switch and, and, she thinks, he comes alive, yes, his voice floats up to the tops of the notes, floats up to the place where the sound really lives, and she hates it, she hates him, when he looks as though he couldn't be happier. And Lori thinks it isn't any wonder she feels it in her stomach. Bile, she thinks, yes, the taste of yellowy brown, and she can't remember the last time she sung a single note, she's far too stiff, she thinks, for all she knows there's something over her windpipe, a film of skin or saliva, yes, there's something stopping the singing from coming up and it takes a certain amount of, reverence, Lori thinks, to grow a sound into a note.

The tone's as fragile as your bog pimpernel, Lo.

And his hair was so thick, his hair came down around his neck, almost as far as his shoulders, and she looks into the fog and she thinks, there's nothing still, no, and she sees the pair of them sitting on the living room floor amongst Joseph's records, twenty, thirty records, she sees the evening light coming in through the window.

She thinks, this has to be the last of the light today, yes, shut up shop, she thinks, and she looks at the records strewn across the carpet and she says if he wants a drink she's pretty sure there's some Martini left. She certainly wouldn't say no to a Martini right now, she could happily have one, if they're going to be sitting here listening to a record or two, and she says she'll bring a couple of glasses through, if he's joining her, and yes, he says, he wouldn't mind a drink either, a Martini would be great and Lori gets up off the floor and goes into the kitchen and she looks over at Joseph sitting amongst his records and she thinks, they don't own much besides clothes, a few books and all these records, no, they really only have enough to get by, which is the way they like it.

Unencumbered. Frictionless, if you like, Lo.

And she thinks, yes, that's the way he likes it, and she opens the cupboard and she thinks, he'll come round to the idea of a car, give him a bit of time, she thinks, and well, she's more than willing to put in a few extra hours at work if it helps them stretch to a little Mini, or even a Morris Marina. She likes the Marinas, the blue ones, she thinks, or damask red and she looks over at Joseph sitting there amongst his records and she thinks, if he isn't contentment itself then she doesn't know, no, she wouldn't know and his hair is as thick as summer bracken. Strong roots, she thinks, and God, she loves him, yes, she almost always wants him. He knew she would, yes, they'd only been together a week when he told her how a sloth that's been shot hangs on to its tree until it decomposes. They've got this vice-like grip, Lo, they literally don't know how to let go, and Lori gets a couple of glasses down from the cupboard and she gets the Martini and she walks back into the living room and now the music is playing. Strings again, Lori thinks, and really she should know, yes, really she should have paid attention when he told her which record he'd chosen, and she thinks, she doesn't listen really, no, she spends all her time looking at him, his hair, she thinks, and she sits down on the carpet and she puts the bottle and the glasses down between them and she thinks, the music isn't nice, no, she can't understand why he doesn't choose something more, and she thinks, more relaxing, yes, once in a while, she thinks, and well, they've gone through this before, the point of music isn't to be nice and she's the first to admit that she doesn't understand a thing, about music.

About the arts, Lo.

And she sits down there on the carpet and she listens to the strings and she thinks, a thick liquid, no, a heavy liquid, that's what she hears and she pours the Martini into the glasses and Joseph takes a glass and she takes the other glass and the pair of them drink the Martini and she looks across the room and out of the window and she thinks, that's just about the last of the evening light then, yes, they're sitting here in the half dark with Martini, with the music slipping in around them like liquid mercury and she thinks, pull the curtains at least, yes, nothing left of the day now and Lori crawls a few feet across the carpet and turns on the little lamp and she gets up and stands at the window and she looks over at the fell on the other side of the valley. The music's too much really, she thinks, she doesn't see why, no, and she pulls the curtains shut and she says they might as well finish off the Martini, yes, why not finish it if there's only this bit left? and she kneels down on the carpet and she pours the rest of the Martini out into the two glasses and she thinks, Martini on a summer's evening and she feels the music slip around her waist, like bone and muscle, and for all she knows she could be tone deaf, no, she hasn't got an ear for it at all, and she looks over at Joe and she thinks she can't help but love him, and she feels the music tighten and she thinks, not tighten, build, Loz, yes, that's what he calls it, and she has to say, not Loz, because who wants to be called, and she thinks, around her lungs, yes, that's where she feels the music and she thinks of the ewe he pulled out from the bog, front legs first, Lori thinks, and for a moment there it looked mid-leap and Lori thinks, a small car will do, a little run-around, something to save them walking down to the main road for the bus. A real country mile that'll be in winter, she thinks, and we'll get him his Bechstein too, she thinks, and she opens her mouth and she feels the air rush back in and she can see from the way he's looking at her.

When he looks at her like that, Lori means, yes, he pulls up a bit on the left. It's almost a smile, she thinks, although not quite, and she pictures his face and she sees the left side pulling up, yes, she thinks, it's always been the left, although now she thinks about it it could just as easily be the other side, no, it hardly looks wrong if she pictures it pulling up on the right side and she thinks, how can't she be sure? How can she be standing here on the fell not knowing which side of his mouth pulls up when she's seen it a thousand times? He can't help it, she thinks, the mouth pulling up, the twinkle wrenched into one eye, and when it comes to her own smile it's frozen itself into a rictus. She's surprised he comes near her still, and well, she doesn't exactly deserve any more than the little peck he gives her before bed, his lips more and more like rubber, like the yellow fingertip of a marigold glove. And Lori thinks, a whole life, moulded into a finger of double-layered latex. Which is another exaggeration, yes, a little inflation here, a little inflation there, she thinks, and his mouth goes up on the left, yes, she was certain it was the left just a moment ago and she thinks of Joseph's face and she pulls his mouth up on the left side again and she pulls it up on the right side. They both work, she thinks, and she takes a long look at his face, and well, she can't really get anything but eyes, floating in a blank face.

Deux yeux flottants, she thinks, if that's how you get an adjective to agree and whenever he starts explaining her mind washes over with black, yes, it's as if everything he tries teaching her is lost in the backflow and if she's told him once, she thinks, because she only has to open her mouth and she anticipates, yes, that's half the problem, she anticipates her own demise, and it isn't just the *r*, it isn't just the diphthongs, the semi-vowels or any of those things, it's the spirit of the language that's lost to her because when she looks out across the valley at the fell she can't so much as conjure up a baguette. Or even a beret, she thinks, no, it's all too far away and Lori pushes her feet over the fell and she thinks, thank God the man and the woman and the dog have gone, and she'll walk a country mile, just one, although she could do with a stick, with something to lean on, she thinks, God knows she's spent enough time conditioning herself into thinking that sticks are for banging. Even this morning she was waiting down-stairs thinking, go on then, bang through, so I know you're alive. She can't escape from it. Bang through, bang through, or does she think don't bang through? isn't that what she really thinks? because she hates the way the vibrations run up through her tibia, she worries about the roof, yes, she can't help looking at the tiles and thinking of teeth in loose sockets, of crowns and necks and roots wincing at every tap. And more than once she's imagined the roof coming down, the pair of them under a pile of mossy rubble. She's imagined Joe tapping with his stick.

SOS.

And always she thinks, you pillock. You fucking pillock. Yes, most of the time, she thinks, and when she woke this morning it wasn't quite light. She stood at the window and looked out at the fell. Her eyes were bad, both of them, she thinks, not just the left, or does she mean the right? and she thinks, no wonder she can't remember which side of his mouth pulls up, and well, the fog had crept down overnight, the tups were out there with the ewes. And this is how she finds herself, in the same place every morning, standing at the window looking down into the gaping mouth of the day ahead, although she never really catches it, that moment before the mind comes alive, no, it's only ever in retrospect, she thinks, because it's easy to get taken up, with a head or something. She picks them up with her bare hands and tosses them into the laurel, and when she scans the flagstones for blood she always thinks, scan quickly, because she doesn't want to think of all the crap. No, once you start, she thinks, and she's always gone on with the belief that the cat licks up the blood, because a little pool would hardly escape her, even a mouse-sized streak, she thinks, although the flagstones hide a multitude, and when it comes to it she couldn't be sure where they keep the mop these days, no, she doesn't know, and she thinks of its little tentacles stiffened up in a cupboard somewhere. Forget about mopping, she thinks, mopping's at the end of the list, although sweeping would help, God, yes, she's seen the bottom of Joe's slippers. She's always surprised how big a crumb seems once it's been flattened. And she thinks, anything but sweeping, which is why she likes to take her time over washing up or making coffee and every morning she prays for Joe to bang through, or is it don't bang through she prays for?

Every morning's the same, Lori thinks, she stands at the window and looks out across the valley whilst she waits for the coffee. Behind the fell is another fell, yes, the fells ripple outwards from their kitchen window, one catastrophe after another, she thinks, and if it wasn't for the *Nine O'Clock News* she'd never see beyond them, no, she'd never get herself over the Pennines, and she thinks, she never has, no, in all this time, and she stands there in the fog and she thinks, 1993, we went to Scarborough, or was it Whitby?

We had fish and chips for dinner, two large cod on the harbour wall, and is that the black dog barking now? Lori thinks, yes, somewhere down there, a big dog's bark, a heavy dog's bark and she has to say that the three of them were really striding out, the man and the woman and the dog. She's hardly surprised they're down there in the valley already and Lori listens to the barking coming in and out of earshot. It's the same when they take the lambs from the ewes each summer. The wailing. She can never escape it even though she can't quite hear it and she thinks, a dog would have changed things, a dog would have gone part way, because she feels a twinge, a little tug of something whenever she sees old John with his collie sitting up next to him in the Land Rover and Lori thinks, Big Ranulph, beautiful Big Ranulph.

Although the truth is that she's never had the energy to campaign for a dog. It took everything she had to get the cat, yes, she fought tooth and nail for the cat and she thinks, thank God she did because the cat's been a real friend over the years, and all of a sudden Lori feels that she wants to be home, yes, the cat will be in for her tea at five, at half past four if she's hungry, and Lori feels a little ache for the cat. Feed the cat at five, she thinks, and she pushes her boots over the sodden earth and well, here she is pressing on over to Sallows when really she needs to be down there with the cat, and she looks down at the bog mosses, the peat, the wet black and she thinks of the droughts she's seen on the news, she thinks of wasted cattle under a relentless sun and she can't imagine, no, she simply hasn't got it in her. Get on home, she thinks, nobody wants to be benighted whilst heading down, no, better to walk up and into the dark and she looks into the fog, and yes, she thinks, the further she walks the less certain her legs are, because where does she feel it? where, if anywhere? and she'll get herself a dog, she'll go on over to the farm in the morning and look for old John, and she thinks, old Lizzie's probably easier to talk to, and well, no, she doesn't know how to talk to either of them, she'll always send Joe round if she's wanting something or other and she thinks, two old blankets in the airing cupboard, a good dog won't need more than that and she thinks, Meg, no, Tess. A dog needs a short name, especially a working dog and she thinks, get going then, yes, because it's been stop-start ever since she shut the front door behind her this morning and Lori thinks, even a tortoise can keep going, yes, the tortoise claws along with its club legs and still wins the race, and she hates Aesop's fables, she's never read one that didn't make her feel bad about herself, and Lori thinks, the fox and the grapes, the crow and the raven. Aesop must've been a right prick, and she thinks, even *Struwwelpeter* wasn't as bad, and well, she won't read now, no, she'll sit with *The Gazette*, but she won't really, she thinks, and the cat will be hungry, the cat will be.

And Lori thinks, cut down to the Garburn then, and she looks into the fog and she looks across the ground in front of her and yes, she thinks, she'll head off the hill after the bracken thins, yes, come down on that little sheep track, and she knows the fell better than anywhere on earth, yes, she's better off up here than in town. Twenty-five years and she still doesn't know how to find the barber's, nor the laundrette.

It's opposite that art shop, love, the one that does frames.

No, she never knows, and if she misses the sheep track she'll have to go up and she thinks, after the bracken thins, yes, she knows it, and she looks into the fog and she thinks, no more barking then, no, the man and the woman and the black dog are long gone and she thinks of the black dog in the back of a car, his paws and his belly towelled down and she pats around herself, she pats down there, rag and bone, she thinks, *Agnus Dei*, and she thinks of Joe at the little window.

Bartók or Ravel? what's your guess then, Lo?

And she thinks, not tears now and she feels them pushing inside her head and she thinks, all day they've been threatening, ever since she stopped on the bridleway and looked up at the sky. White from end to end, yes, that's how it was this morning, Lori thinks, and it's been nothing but rain all month, one rain after another rain, there's hardly been time to breathe between them and she looks across the rough ground and she feels the tears pushing inside and she thinks, there can't be another landscape that takes the rains like this one, that absorbs violence after violence and in summer gives flowers that wear veins in their petals. Bog pimpernel, Lori thinks, skylarks, cottongrass.

It really is only a small light, a November light, but still,
Lori thinks, and she comes down another few steps, yes, a
few steps at a time will do it, slow and steady wins the race.
And she thinks, come on down now, come home against
the light, and as long as there are November afternoons,
she thinks, yes, as long as there are November afternoons
she wants to be coming home. And Lori comes down a
few more steps and at last she sees the valley opening up
beneath her and she thinks, it's a thin light for sure, but
there, everything's the way it's always been, and she looks
down into the valley, she looks at the thin lines of the beck,
the bridleway that runs on past Long Green Head to the
Tongue and she feels something swell inside her. And
when she gets to the Garburn she'll have what's left of the
scones, yes, even scones will taste good, she thinks, and
she shuffles down a few more steps and she says, step by
step, and she doesn't notice whether her voice shakes or
doesn't shake and she looks down into the valley and she
thinks, Emile shot a crow down from the sky. That was too
long ago, and now the light is so thin, a thread of light,
yes, the year's almost done. And Lori thinks, O come all ye
faithful. She thinks, O come all ye faithful, and she shuffles down a few more steps and yes, she thinks, it's some
kind of a miracle, the valley spilling out from the fog and
she thinks, Joyful and triumphant, although the light is
so thin it can hardly be called light and the day Emile took
the air rifle from the shed it was summer, summertime,
Lori thinks, there was light from the first to the last and
she went next door to look in on the baby because nothing

was happening with Joseph and her, no, she'd given up on anything happening between them a long time before baby Fergus came along, and she walked the few steps along the lane. So much light, Lori thinks, the way it always is in summer, and foxgloves, yes, a ditch crammed with purples and greens, and she comes down a few more steps and she thinks, the walls inside the house were almost cold, yes, she had her hand flat against the wall in the stairwell and she thinks, let it all come back. It can't hurt now, not after all this time and Lori shuffles down a few more steps. The legs don't want to, she thinks, no, the further she comes, and she stood at the top of the stairs and looked the length of the landing. How did they all fit in there, she thinks, all nine of them? the place is no bigger than their own little house, and it's as if she's thinking all this for the first time although she's thought it so many times, over and over she thinks it and Lori thinks, there's music in that, yes, there's music in all of it. Slippers on the kitchen floor, she thinks, dust and scratches, yes, wasn't he always saying? and she looks down into the tired valley and she thinks, of all the arts, yes, that's what she thinks, of all the arts, music is the one that reaches, and she pushed open the door, she saw the baby's basket at the foot of the bed and she thinks, you can't be sure what you remember and what you invent and she walked over to the window. She stood at the window too long, it was almost cold by then, the wind had brought the clouds in off the fells and Lori thinks, far too long, standing doing nothing, and she comes down a few more steps towards the stile that separates the fell from the Pass and when she brings the record player down from the loft she'll choose *Fratres*, yes, that's what she wants to listen to. Pärt before Bach, although Bach too, yes, the hours he spent listening were good hours, she thinks, and once in a rare while the sound of Glenn Gould humming whilst he played, and yes, Lori thinks, you can get used to having so much, you can become almost, and she thinks, keep on with the milkman, yes, she'll put out for a pint every other day, which is hardly anything but it might be too much still, and she thinks, her legs.

She's always thought the legs would outlive the rest of the body, but she's wrong on that one too, yes, she looked inside the basket, she remembers the light blue blanket, the baby with a head, a face, and when she goes to kiss him she thinks, no, because the baby's dead. Although he wasn't dead, that wasn't the day he died, no, that was the day Emile killed the crow, and she thinks, Felix and Emile grew up in front of her eyes, she's watched courgettes grow more slowly, and she takes a few more steps down towards the stile and she thinks, all those children, seventeen years between the first and the last of them, and Fergus was only sleeping that day, yes, the day he died was weeks after she leant over the basket, weeks after the kiss, if there was a kiss, she thinks, and well, no, there wasn't ever a kiss.

They'd woken to thick rain.

Lori waited on the coffee whilst Joe put the bucket out in the back room. The rain kept on past breakfast, past noon, and all she could think was thank God, because she'd wanted a day with an empty yard, yes, she'd wanted rain above everything else and well, the rain kept coming, Lori thinks, the yard stayed empty. Some time around one she started on the soup, she took onions, celery, carrots from the vegetable rack. The carrots had almost gone over, she thinks, and the black-handled knife was still in the sink, yes, she'd pulled pale ham from the plughole, she'd turned the radio on. She'd turned it off again. No, she'd thought, and she'd rinsed the knife under running water, her finger and thumb up and down the blade and outside the rain was really coming down, yes, the village was sitting under a dark lid of sky.

It didn't have to be Fergus, Lori thinks, she always thinks, it didn't have to be, because she was ready to go herself, she'd got herself down as far as hips and ribs, she'd got herself past the horror of seeing too much hair in the drain, God, yes, she was down to her peninsular collarbone, cheekbones, too many bones and she thinks, the skipping ropes and sticks, the little pairs of wellies, the shouting, the pushing, the making up tasted like poison. All of it, Lori thinks, yes, it started with Felix and Emile. Then Ross, then Charlotte, Louise, Silas, memories heaped on stagnant memories, she thinks, and she comes down a few more steps, she comes down with weak legs and she thinks, the rain was heavy that day, so heavy the chickens hadn't come out for their feed, no, the yard was empty and she'd thought, thank God, thank God. With alarming fervour, Lori thinks, yes, she'd sliced the air above the kitchen sink with the black-handled knife, once, twice, it sounded so clean it was difficult to stop. The sound of violence, Lori thinks. The body obeys without thinking, even a half body like hers, and well, she had a few carrots, she had some celery, an onion, she had enough for soup, she thinks, and she'd spent the whole summer shrinking under her nylon blouses whilst Felix, Emile and Ross worked over at the farm, their arms and backs and faces more and more permanent, and she thinks, the girls, Silas out there in the yard and then the baby, yes, the seventh one and she'd started with an onion, she'd stood it on its root end and listened to the rainwater collecting in the bucket and she'd thought, thank God, because the yard was empty, the lane was empty, fat pellets were floating in the chicken trough.

And now Lori sees Annie.

Yes, here we go, Lori thinks, this again and she says, step by step, step by step and she feels how much she's shaking, yes, she's really shaking too much, she thinks, get yourself down and over the stile then stop and eat what's left of the scones, yes, get something inside you, she thinks, and she shuffles down a few more steps.

And she sees herself standing at the kitchen counter with the black-handled knife, she sees the onion on the chopping board and outside in the yard she sees Annie, she sees her as clear as day, the way she always does and still she doesn't understand what she's seeing, no, she never seems to understand why she sees Annie running across the yard with the baby, because the rain is really coming down, the rain hasn't let up all day.

And Lori says, step by step, she says, step by step, and she feels her heart coming back, yes, here it comes, she thinks, and she presses her hand against her chest and she sees that her hand is shaking too much, that really she's gone too far with the shaking, although she can't be all that cold, no, there have been colder days, far colder, she thinks, yes, thick plates of ice and she looks across the valley and she sees that the sky has settled over the land like a huge slab of stone, or slate, she thinks, and she feels it pressing down and she thinks, just get yourself off here, yes, get yourself

down to the stile and she comes down a few more steps
and she thinks, scones are for warm afternoons, yes, scones
are for china plates and she can't even guess how long she's
been out, it might not be noon yet, yes, for all she knows
it could still be morning, and if it is she's still got time
to get something done today, she's still got time to get the
Chambéry out to the shed and she comes down another
step and the sky presses down, yes, a huge sky after all,
she thinks.

And Lori sees Annie out there in the yard with the baby,
and she sees the thick rain coming down, the rain doesn't
stop coming, Lori thinks, and she leans against the kitchen
counter with the black-handled knife and the onion and
the thick rain keeps coming and well, the bucket will soon
be full, she thinks, it'll hardly take long for the bucket to fill
if the rain keeps coming like this, and Lori leans against
the kitchen counter and she hears Joseph on the stairs and
she can't understand why he's hurrying. No need to hurry,
she thinks, and she slices the onion and she thinks, one
onion might not be enough and she looks out into the yard
and she sees the rain and she sees Joseph out there with
Annie and she thinks, you could shut the door Joe, it
doesn't take much effort to shut a door and she puts down
the knife and she thinks, if he's going to run around the
place like a wild animal she'll shut it herself and she looks
at the carrots and she thinks, they've almost gone over, yes,
without carrots the soup will be nothing and she goes to
shut the back door and she stands in the porch and she
sees Joseph out there in the rain with Annie and she sees
that Annie's carrying a doll after all, yes, the rain is running
down its hard face, she thinks, and Lori takes a pair of

boots from the rack, she puts them on and steps out
into the yard, she stands in the rain and looks out beyond
the laurel, although no, she thinks, the clouds have shut
down the valley and the fell and here we all are getting wet,
Joseph, Annie with a doll, and the rain is so thick, yes,
she feels it slide over her scalp and down her neck and
she thinks, Medusa, yes, with a head full of snakes and she
hears Joseph call her name and she thinks, wait, just wait
and it can't be Persimmon who beheads Medusa, no, not
Persimmon, and well, she doesn't read enough to know,
she should read a bit more, she should take down some of
Joseph's books, and she hears Joseph call her name and she
thinks, the books smell, that's why she doesn't, and she
hears Joseph call and she thinks, nobody's interested in the
Gorgon, no, forget the Gorgon and get inside and phone for
an ambulance, yes, that's what he's saying, shouting almost
and the rain is coming down, sheets of rain and at last we
need an ambulance, after all these years of playing in the
yard it's time for an ambulance, and well, yes, Joseph's right,
someone should go inside and phone and she thinks, a
persimmon's a fruit with sweet, sweet flesh and she looks
at Annie and the doll over there in the rain and she thinks,
not a doll, no, not a doll after all, and Joseph says go, and
he waves his arm and Lori says, yes, yes, and she feels her
wet blouse against her flat breasts, her ribs and she thinks,
yes, go on in and she steps inside the porch and shuts the
door and every time it rains like this she thinks the gutter
needs doing, yes, listen to that, she thinks, and she thinks,
boots off, she doesn't want wet about the place and she
takes the boots off and puts them back on the rack and she
goes on into the living room and she thinks, phone now,
yes, they're waiting for you to phone and she hears the

rainwater dripping into the bucket and she thinks, the
bucket must almost be full because the rain hasn't stopped
coming all morning. Joseph won't have seen to it, no, it's
enough to get him to put it out, she thinks, and she'll take
a moment to check on the bucket, yes, first she'll check
on the bucket and she walks on into the back room and she
thinks, oh no, not Fergus, not that little one, and she sees
that Joseph has put a towel down under the bucket, yes,
he's put one of the nice bath towels down on the dirty floor
and she thinks, it isn't on, using one of the nice bath towels
to soak up the rainwater, not when we've got a box of old
rags in the store and how many times has she told him?
take the rags, take the bloody, and she looks at the towel
spread out over the dirty floor and she thinks, leave it, she
can't do anything with a dirty towel now, no, the towel can
go in with tomorrow's wash, and she thinks, check the
bucket, yes, that's why she's here, the rain's falling in sheets
out there, and she goes over to the bucket and she sees that
it's only half full, that it won't need emptying for a while at
least and that's one less job to do, yes, she can forget about
the bucket for a bit and Lori thinks, well, now she should
go through and phone, and she walks back into the living
room and she stands by the little brown table, the table
where the phone sits and she thinks again that it's a funny
table, a table with three legs, and her stomach doesn't feel
quite right, no, her stomach feels almost hot and she thinks,
there's something wrong, yes, she's too weak, she's got
herself down to hips and ribs in front of his eyes and she
pulls up her wet blouse and puts her hand against her
stomach and she thinks, my God, because where has the
other half of her gone? and she looks around the living
room and no, she thinks, you won't be finding yourself

here, love, and she picks up the receiver and she thinks, not a doll after all, no, for a moment there she'd thought, and it isn't as if they haven't had rain like this before, no, they get rain like this all the time and she thinks, what's rain got to do with anything? then Joseph shouted at her, almost shouted, she thinks, and of course she knows it's Perseus who beheaded Medusa, only a coward comes up on some-one whilst they're sleeping, yes, and she puts her finger in the dial, let everything unravel, she thinks, and she turns and looks out of the window into the yard and she sees them standing there in the rain, Annie and Joe. No, she thinks, and she puts the receiver back down. No, the baby's dead anyway.

And Lori goes back outside and she sees that Felix and Emile have come out into the yard and she thinks, where's Annie? where's she gone now? and she sees Annie sitting on the ground under the woodpile roof and she sees her rocking and rocking with baby Fergus in her arms and she thinks, well, at least they're dry under there because the rain is almost as heavy as it gets and she walks over to Joseph, to Felix and Emile, and she says that the ambulance won't be long, and she says it again, the ambulance will soon be here, yes, she says, hold on. And a wind comes across the yard, a wind pushes at the rain, and Joseph tells Felix and Emile to go out onto the lane and wait for the ambulance, and Felix and Emile walk out onto the lane and the wind comes one more time, pushing at the rain and Lori says, yes, the ambulance won't be long now, and after Lori has said that there is only rain and the sound that's been coming from Annie. The way blood comes, Lori thinks, and she says, yes, the ambulance is on its way everybody and she says, everybody, everybody, and Joseph walks out onto the lane and he walks back over to the woodpile and around the yard, he looks over at the wall of cloud and he says, it's taking too long, and he kicks at the laurel and the rain comes down and he says he should've taken them in the car, the car would've been a damn sight quicker, he says, and he'll get his keys, he'll go on in, and no, Lori says, no, the ambulance will be here soon and Joseph steps forwards and backwards, he steps forwards and backwards and the wind comes again, it pushes a film of water across the yard, and at least Annie and the baby are under the woodpile roof, Lori thinks, yes, at least the baby is more or less dry, and Joseph walks around the yard, he walks past the chicken shed, the cherry tree, he walks back to the woodpile and he steps forwards, he steps backwards and he says to Lori, phone again, go in and phone again, and Lori goes back inside and yes, she's glad to go back in because there was only the rain, she thinks, and the sound coming out from Annie, and she thinks, now it will leak down into the valley, yes, now the sound will stain the valley and she walks over to the table, the funny table with three legs and she picks up the receiver and she thinks perhaps she will be sick, that if there's anything left inside her it's about to come out and she takes a couple of breaths and she puts her finger in the dial and sooner or later someone on the other end says, which service do you require?

And now Lori reaches the stile.

Yes, here we are at last, she thinks, and she looks out over the stile and she sees that the whole of the valley has appeared, that nothing has changed after all and she pulls herself up and over the stile and she sees the valley stretching out below, she sees all her familiar places.

And she thinks, sit and eat what's left of the scones now, although there can't be much more than a handful of crumbs, no, she's gone over and over it with the scones, she thinks, and she says, just eat, and she sits herself down on the verge and she puts her hand inside her pocket.

And now this onion has been sitting here since noon, Lori thinks, yes, she should have dealt with the onion before now and she picks up the chopping board and the black-handled knife and she scrapes the onion into the bin and well, that's one less job, she thinks, and she hears the rain-water dripping into the bucket, and well, yes, the bucket, she'd almost forgotten about the bucket and she can hardly leave it all night, can she? no, someone needs to tackle the bucket before bed, she thinks, and that really is the last thing she feels like doing right now, skulking around in the back room. She doesn't know why they don't get a light put in. We just don't, she thinks, and when the ambulance took Annie and Fergus away Emile was sick in the ditch on the far side of the lane and she'll do the bucket, if they've got this rain all night the bucket won't wait until morning, she thinks, and she looks at Joe over there in his chair and she thinks, there's nothing to be got from sitting all day, no, get yourself moving and help with the bucket can't you? yes, get up now, get up and draw the curtains at least.

And Lori eats a handful of crumbs.

The scones are really past it, she thinks, and well, she wouldn't be eating scones that taste like this if she'd made herself a proper breakfast, yes, she'd have got a lot further along with an omelette, she thinks, a bowl of porridge or something, and she watches her hand move towards her mouth and she thinks, you can just stop shaking and eat, Lori Fitzgerald, and she doesn't get used to it, does she? she's been shaking on and off for years and still she's surprised when she looks down at her hand and sees it misbehaving and she thinks, eat now and she sees the sugar spilling over the edge of the counter and across the flagstones and she sees it lying there like splinters of glass, and of course Annie was expecting again, she was hoping for a little girl after all those boys and she didn't want anything more than a couple of hundred grams of sugar for the early apples. All Lori had to do was pour the sugar, get the sugar into the bowl, but she was shaking from head to toe.

And Lori watches as Annie crosses the yard with the bowl of sugar, she watches as she goes in through the back door, as Felix and Emile and little Ross run in after her. And the sugar has spilt, yes, the sugar is all over the kitchen floor and Lori thinks, get the broom out, yes, go on, fetch the broom and she goes to the cupboard and she pulls out the broom and she sees that her arms are trembling, that her arms are still shaking and she thinks, calm down, can't you? and she grips the broom as hard as she can and she thinks, hold it steady at least and she says, congratulations, congratulations, congratulations again. Congratulations, congratulations, congratulations and she thinks, just hold the broom steady, and she sees that the sun is catching hold of the sugar down there on the flagstones, yes, look at that, she thinks, and she starts to sweep and she says, congratulations then, yes, congratulations, and if you can't hold the broom steady. If you can't even do that, she thinks, and she sees the broom bumping over the flagstones and she says it again, congratulations, and the broom bumps and she thinks, why don't you just sweep, just sweep the sugar up? No, it's hardly too much to ask, and she looks at her dress and she thinks, the dress has too much colour, yes, what's she doing in a dress like this when summer's so far along, what's she doing in pinks and reds and yellows?

And she pushes the broom over the flagstones and she thinks, she can't get anything right, can she? No, she can't even sweep up her own mess without the broom skidding and bumping and she thinks, how exciting, next door are expecting, they're hoping for a little girl, congratulations, congratulations and she thinks, stop saying congratulations and she says, congratulations and she thinks, shut up, and the broom skids and bumps and Lori sits herself down on the kitchen floor. The air smells of cut grass still, Lori thinks, yes, ever since morning and now the sugar has scattered everywhere, yes, now she's down here on the flagstones in her summer dress.

Felix, Emile, Ross, and another one wasn't exactly part of the plan, no, a bit of a shock, all a bit of a.

And Lori takes the broom and she pushes the handle up under her dress, she pushes it up between her legs and she thinks, hold your arms still, can't you? And she feels the broom nudging up there and she thinks, go on then, and the broom nudges and the afternoon sun falls across the flagstones, yes, the sugar, like glass now, almost sparkling and she feels the broom handle and she thinks, go on, yes, go on, if you've got anything about you at all, and the window is wide open, the sun is pouring in, and out in the yard she hears the boys, Felix, Emile, Ross and expecting now, hoping for a little girl and she thinks, if you're putting it up, and she feels the tip of the broom inside her and she says, congratulations, congratulations then, and isn't she sick of fingers? yes, hasn't she had too much of fingers and the shame she feels when they come out wet? no, the body doesn't care, she thinks, the body doesn't know what's missing and she pushes at the broom, yes, stick that up you, ram that up you, and now she's pushing, yes, now she's going, out then in so hard she feels something open.

And there now, she thinks, the boys in the yard, the sun on the flagstones and she wipes the blood the length of her thigh and she thinks, dear God, dear God, because whatever she does it still doesn't hurt enough.

The home stretch, she thinks, and she takes a few steps
down the track, yes, step by step, she thinks, and she looks
over at their little house on the other side of the valley and
she thinks, all she really needs to do when she gets in is
feed the cat, yes, the cat's the one thing that can't wait, she
thinks, and she can put down a few biscuits and if there's
enough left in the legs she can wheel the *Chambéry* out to
the shed, and Lori pushes her feet over the loose stones
and she thinks, home is where the heart is, and she walks
on down into the valley and she thinks, the light has almost
gone, yes, the small November light, and she hears a sound
coming from the other side of the valley. The black dog
again, she thinks, but no, the black dog is long gone, the
dog will be having his tea by now, she thinks, and she
pushes her feet over the loose stones and she thinks, if you
can just stop dragging, and well, no, she thinks, she can't,
and she hears the sound again, she hears it coming across
the valley and she thinks, hardly a dog, no, nothing like a
dog, and she stands there on the track and listens. Singing,
she thinks, yes, somebody's singing over there and she
thinks, Schubert, yes, she knows it, she knows it as well
as she knows the ground beneath her feet, and she thinks,
dear Joe, darling Joe. I'm coming, yes, just a few steps
behind you, and she pushes her feet over the stones and
she hears the singing and she thinks, it's ridiculous, it's too
much to believe and she leans in to the valley and she hears
the song coming out exactly as she expects it to, yes, note
after note, exactly as she expects it, and yes, she knows this
song, she loves this song and she feels Joseph's arm around
her back and she feels his hand on her shoulder and she

thinks, OK, yes, we'll walk together for a while and Joseph and Lori walk down into the valley. Schubert, she says, and well, she knows it, yes, she knows, and Lori looks down into the valley and she looks at the village sitting under its stone sky. We had it all, she thinks, yes, everything anyone could want from a life, and she feels Joseph's hand on her shoulder, she feels his arm around her back and she thinks, let's go on home then, and the pair of them walk down the track and as they walk the wind brings the singing across the valley, and she thinks, get yourself up into the attic and bring the record player down, yes, she'll get the record player going again and she says, we're all TV these days Joe, and if truth be known she's never seen any point in the TV after the headlines are done and doesn't she always get cold? doesn't she always? although she never believed her legs would turn, no, the legs have always been enough, she thinks, and they bought the house, they bought a Morris Marina too, they ran it until the clutch finally went and somehow they arrived at one car for him and one for her. The bike, she thinks, the TV, the microwave, things get added on, and you don't know where along the line it happens. Like weight around the middle, Lori thinks, although how can she say a thing about weight when she looks the way she does? and they've got tennis rackets and golf clubs, they've got a good set of knives, a Commodore 64 under the chair in the porch. A toaster, a carriage clock, a pair of gold rings, they've got shoes for going out, wine for staying in, two rear cassettes waiting in the outdoor loo, and she thinks, waiting for what? And she feels Joseph's arm around her shoulder. We'll go on down, let's go on down now, she thinks, and the sky has settled over the valley like a huge slab of slate, and still the singing comes, Lori thinks, and she feels Joseph's hand in hers, yes, hands can be good and bad, she thinks, the same hands. And aren't they almost down already? yes, aren't they almost at the point of? and she thinks, yes, she'll be turning right when the track forks, it'll be down past Howe Farm to the bridge for her, and she looks back up the track and she looks down the bridleway that leads to the bridge. Go on then Joe, she says, you'd better be going on, and she feels his hand leave hers and she thinks, Schubert, yes, that was a good one and she drags her feet over the loose stones and she thinks, the singing can't have come over on the wind, no, there's only been the tiniest of winds all day, none at all really, and the day Emile shot the crow it had been almost hot.

Silas wrapped it in his T-shirt and she watched from the window as he carried it up from the valley. The clouds were already coming over, Lori thinks, yes, the wind was already bringing the clouds off the fells and by the time she'd decided to go next door the heat had almost gone, yes, she'd stood at the window and watched the clouds come over whilst baby Fergus slept. The rain came soon afterwards, Lori thinks, it came in fat drops and muddied the dust in the yard. She put the bucket out in the back room and when Joseph got home from work she said they really ought to get a light fixed up out there before the clocks go back, yes, they were talking about the light when Felix appeared at the window.

And Lori says, Joseph, Joe.

Joe, she says, Felix's there at the window, and Joseph gets up from his chair and goes over to the window.

Come to the door, lad, he says, get yourself under the porch where it's dry, and Joseph goes to the door and opens it and Lori sees Felix come and stand under the porch and she looks at the rain coming down all around him and she thinks, at least he's dry a moment, yes, let the lad dry off a moment.

Silas, Felix says, mam was just wondering if you've seen Silas, and Joseph says, Silas, no, no, we've not seen him and he looks over at Lori and Lori shakes her head and a big gust of wind throws the rain against the side of the house and Joseph says, stand yourself inside a moment, lad, and Felix turns and looks out into the rain.

Mam's got his tea on the table, that's all, he says, and Lori looks at Felix standing there under the porch and she thinks, how much trouble can there be in a day? is there really no end to the amount of trouble? because it's only been hours since Emile killed the crow, since she hung her head over the baby's basket and Felix says, it'll be getting cold, his tea, and Joseph says they'll go and get Silas now, not to worry.

And yes, Lori thinks, Joseph's always known how to talk to Felix and Emile and she watches Joe take his jacket from the hook, she watches him take his boots from the rack and she hears the garden gate open then shut and she thinks, the door Joe, it wouldn't hurt to shut the door, although no, who cares about the door? she thinks, she can hardly make herself care about something like that and she holds her hands out in front of her. She's nothing more than a skeleton, yes, she's got these bulbous knuckles now and she turns them palm down and she thinks, they'll flower, yes, perhaps she'll spring snowdrops out of all this trouble and when she shuts her eyes she almost always sees it, a flesh-boring insect tunnelling beneath the skin on her hips, her ribs, her spine, cleaning her down to nothing but bone, and well, it doesn't take much, no, it only takes one thing to eat away at you, a single borer, a single larva to girdle and kill a small tree. If the tree's susceptible, Lori thinks, and she walks over to the record player and lifts the lid. Arvo Pärt again. Yes, first it was *Tabula Rasa* and now it's this *Fratres*, yes, we'll have to listen to *Fratres* over and over until he's satisfied, and she hears the rain coming down outside and she can say with certainty that she's never put on a record herself. He hasn't let her near the thing, not once in all these years, she thinks, and she looks at the record player's tiny red light and she thinks, he never turns the bloody thing off. And it's raining so hard out there. Cats and dogs and she lifts the arm of the record player between her finger and thumb and lets the needle down onto the black vinyl.

Fratres, Lori thinks, and the music falls out from the speakers into the living room the way it always does, yes, we're used to music in here, she thinks, we've had music ever since the day we moved in and she listens to the music the way Joseph taught her, note after note she listens and she imagines Joe saying, find the line, hear the line, and she imagines him tracing the line, painting the line. You pillock, she thinks, you pretentious pillock, and the wind throws a fistful of rain at the window and she thinks, Silas isn't down in the valley, no, a boy his age is never down in the valley and she listens to the music and she thinks, isn't there more than the line anyway? yes, the thing she hears is more like a belly, a heavy cog that holds everything together, and well, she wouldn't know, no, she doesn't know and she listens to the music turn its clean circle, she listens to the rain and she looks out of the open door and across the valley at the black fell. Autumn's got his fingers around the end of summer already, she thinks, and she walks into the porch and she gets her boots down from the rack and her jacket from the hook and she thinks, the dust and scratches add life, yes, and she steps down into the yard and walks a few steps towards the low fence and she thinks, now there's another baby, now there's this seventh one, this last one on top of all the others and she thinks, it'll never last, the breaths it takes are so small, no, she's never seen anyone take less than their fair share in life. And Lori looks out into the black. Nothing but, she thinks, and the wind brings a ball of rain across the yard and she thinks, relax, yes, because Joseph knows how to talk to those boys next door. She's thought that so many times, yes, she thought it the day they moved in even, and she stands in the yard and she pictures little Felix all those years ago, she pictures him crossing next-door's yard with Marsalis in his arms. He carried that cat from the woodpile to the fence, she thinks, and she pictures Marsalis's legs hanging down and she remembers little Felix saying, here's Marsalis. Joseph went down on his haunches. He stroked Marsalis between the ears, and she thinks, he must have said something to Felix, yes, hasn't he always known exactly what to say to the boys? and she pictures Joseph down there on his haunches with his hair almost at his shoulders and she thinks, perhaps he didn't say anything at all because in all honesty he's never been one for talking, and the rain is really coming down this evening, Lori thinks, and she stands in the yard and she hears the rain falling all around her, she hears it far away and she hears it running onto the back roof in a thick stream and she thinks they'll have to fix the break in the gutter before autumn gets hold, and she steps over the low fence and she stands in the next-door yard.

And now they have seven, she thinks. One, two, three, four, five, six, seven, and she supposes that will be it, seven, yes, seven is enough for anyone, and this afternoon Emile killed the crow and now Silas is missing and the rain is hammering and it hammers so often, Lori thinks. We hardly get a run of days without rain, and she stands there in the yard looking out into the black and she says, Silas, and she loves that name, Silas, it's her favourite, she thinks, and only this afternoon she watched as he came up from the valley with the crow in his T-shirt and Lori walks over to the chicken shed and she knocks on the door and she says, Silas, Silas, and she pushes at the door a little bit, she pushes it open a tiny bit and she says, OK, she's coming in now, if he doesn't mind, she'll just come in and sit in with him for a while because the rain's really coming down out here, and Lori gets down on her hands and knees and she crawls in through the wooden door and she sees Silas over there on the other side of the shed and she says she'll just sit here, sit in the corner for a while if he doesn't mind, and well, it's nice and dry in here, it's a good place to be when the rain's hammering and Lori sits in the corner with her knees up against her chest and she thinks, well, yes, it smells quite a bit, but it's OK, it's really quite safe in here with the chickens and she says she'll sit here for a while, if that's OK with him, with you, Silas, and well, Silas doesn't have much to say, no, nothing's changed there, she thinks, and she likes a quiet one, yes, she falls for the quiet ones often enough and the pair of them are sitting in the shed with the chickens and the rain is really hammering, it's really coming down out there and she supposes the music has stopped now, she supposes Joseph and Felix are down in the valley and well, Joseph will know what to say to Felix,

Joseph will have the right words, she thinks, and she'll just let them go on looking for Silas, calling for Silas, because it hardly matters if his tea gets cold this once, Lori thinks, no, they'll just sit in here for a while, Lori and Silas, yes, they'll just sit in with the chickens, and well, there isn't much light in here but she can make out the chickens, four chickens settled on the perch, she can make out Silas over there in his shorts and she thinks, it's too cold for him to be wearing shorts now, although it was warm enough this afternoon, it was almost hot, she thinks, and she pictures Silas coming up from the valley carrying the dead crow. The clouds were already on their way over, she thinks, and she supposes the clouds must have built right up because now the rain is really coming down, and she watched as Silas laid the crow on the woodpile and she thinks, he must have gone back to get it later, yes, because by the time she looked out from the baby's bedroom window he was sitting on the ground with his hand resting on the crow's head and why did she go along next door? she thinks, why do that when there was already trouble in the air? and the crow went down on the second shot, yes, it only took two, Lori thinks, and she looks over at Silas and she says, Silas, Silas, and now the chickens have settled for the night, yes, everything's the way it usually is, Lori thinks, and she looks at Silas sitting there in his shorts and she thinks, there was blood after all, yes, his shorts are stained. Annie will have a job getting blood out of those, yes, cold water and salt for blood, and she says, why not sit here for a while longer? yes, why not sit in with the chickens for a while and if Silas wants to go on stroking the crow, well that's fine, because the rain is really coming down out there, and in all truth they're probably better off in here anyway, better off where it's dry.

And Lori watches as Silas strokes the crow from its head to the end of its tail feathers and she thinks, yes, stroke the crow, and the crow lies there across Silas's bare knees and well, he should probably be getting on in for his tea now, yes, his mam will be worried sick already, and the crow lies across his knees, the crow is so still and Lori thinks, yes, go gently with the crow and she watches Silas's hand move from the crow's head to the end of its tail feathers and thank God she put the bucket out earlier because the rain is really coming down out there, it's about as bad as it gets, she thinks, and Lori looks over at Silas. Here we all are, she thinks, as safe as houses, yes, Silas, the chickens, the crow, and, and me, and yes, there's always been something with Silas. He makes chains from daisies, Lori thinks, he sits out there on the verge in the lane. For hours and hours, yes, hours and hours of slitting and threading and really he's only a small boy, he can't be older than seven or eight, but that's how it is with Silas, she thinks, and she's spent enough time working out in the yard herself this summer, yes, the pair of them are out there together often enough, Silas in the lane, Lori in the yard, and well, they're almost done with summer now, yes, they're up to their last long days out there, she thinks, and well, they've only just got to know each other, yes, they've been out there all summer, Lori with the veg and Silas with his daisies and it's only been a few days since he came on over, yes, late one afternoon he got up from the verge and walked over to the low fence and Lori had thought, well, here comes Silas at last, and he stood at the low fence holding a long string of daisies, he stood there for a while, quite a while, she thinks, and nothing happened, no, nothing else happened. But still, Lori thinks, and Silas is stroking the crow from the top of its head to the end of its tail feathers, Silas passes his hand over and over the crow and the rain is coming down onto the roof of the chicken shed. It doesn't stop, Lori thinks, and Silas walked over, he stood by the low fence whilst she worked in the yard, and she thinks of his daisies, and she thinks of his bare arms and his bare legs and she thinks, they were baling out in the fields that day.

LORI WALKS DOWN INTO THE VALLEY UNDER THE HEAVY SKY

A huge slab of slate, or sandstone, she thinks, and she pushes her boots over the loose stones. There isn't much to be done about the shaking once it's found its way in, no, she'll just have to keep on going the way she's going, shaking or no shaking, and she makes her way over the loose stones and she feels the sky pressing, yes, pressing on her head and on her chest and she thinks, it's far too late in the day for exaggerating. You'd think she would have learned, and well, no, she thinks, some things you never learn and she looks up at the sky and she feels, yes, a heavy slab of stone there on her chest and she looks over to the east and she looks over to the west and she sees a small patch of blue and well, she'd hardly expected that today, no, it's been nothing but slog since she set out this morning, nothing but stop-start since she shut the garden gate and well, now there's this break in the clouds, now there's this little patch of blue and she thinks, hooray, she thinks, hip hip, and she pushes her boots over the stones and if she isn't lighter on her feet already, if she isn't almost striding again, and she's been all over the place today, yes, it's all come back to her today, and she thinks, Felix and Emile, she thinks, Fergus, she thinks, the black dog will be sleeping somewhere warm, and of course she knows Silas is Joseph's son, well yes, she's always known that, although she forgets.

None of it really matters now, she thinks, not in the grand scheme of things because she'd already decided she loved Silas anyway, yes, that was already done, she thinks, and she looks up at the sky, she looks across at the small patch of blue and she thinks, of all good things, yes, of all beautiful things and she pushes her boots over the loose stones and she says, Joseph, Joe.

Joe, she says. And all the things that matter disappear in the end, Lori thinks, even the things that turn in circles, the ones you think will go on turning and she thinks, *Fratres*, she thinks, any music, all music, yes, it all finishes the same way and she opens her mouth and she thinks, not yet, no, but sooner or later she'll manage a little song and in the morning she'll go along to the farm, she'll speak to old Lizzie and once she's taken the *Chambéry* out to the shed there'll be enough space in the kitchen. A couple of old blankets under the kitchen table will be enough for a dog. Brake callipers, speed shifters. A rear derailleur on the bread bin and she feels sick, yes, now she feels and she thinks, no. No, no, there's nothing to be sick on, there isn't anything more to bring up than a bit of scone and she thinks, sky above, heavens above, and they settled on racing green for the Morris Marina, he put his hand up her skirt whilst he drove it down The Struggle.

We'll stop for a pint at the Golden Rule.

We'll play some vinyl when we get home.

Bach, Britten, Berg. And the year's gone by, yes, she only has to blink, she thinks. And these last leaves hang well into December, yes, there'll be decorations about the village before the last leaves come down and she thinks, O come, she thinks, O come let us adore him, and she pushes her boots over the loose stones and Joe.

Joe, you daft bugger, Joseph, Joe, four dead bodies is too many. Yes, her heart's shrivelled to the size of four. Because when it comes to bodies without names, when it comes to the dead piled on the dead on the other side of their glass screen she couldn't care less, no, the Brixton bomb, she thinks, the Kosovo war, she starts on the washing up, she starts with the pot and pans.

Get the worst over with, love, that's the thing.

And of all of them, Fergus was the worst. His legs hung. His face was so hard she'd thought he was a doll, and she thinks of hanging legs and leaves. Lies, she thinks, and doesn't she always insist on making a mountain where there's a mountain to be made? She won't change, no, too late for change all round.

LORI LEANS AGAINST THE STONE WALL AT THE BOTTOM OF THE BRIDLEWAY

The valley's the same as ever, she thinks, yes, this is how the valley is so late in the year, and she sees the tups over there with the ewes, she sees the crows and the jackdaws and she thinks, everything's the way it should be, yes, everything's in order, and well, now she needs to stop leaning on the wall and get herself up the bridleway. One last push, that's all it needs, a final push, and she'll make herself coffee before she does anything else, because more often than not she starts the day with two, yes, she follows up the first mug with another mug, and she feels the wet down there, she feels the cold and she thinks, one last push, a final push, because their little house is just up there, a stone's throw away and she turns and looks back and she sees the fog lining the fell and she thinks, everything's the way it should be, no, there's nothing to be told from the earth alone and she looks down and sees the water trickling through the stones, she sees the water making its way down into the valley, and well, the rain's really been coming down of late. Whole days and nights of rain, she thinks, and if she's got enough left in her legs after feeding the cat she'll get the *Chambéry* out to the shed. One last job. And she thinks, a country mile, she thinks, one small step for a man. And Joe wasn't quite right last night, that's what he said, and she'd thought, thank God, when he went upstairs, yes go on up, get on up, and isn't it sod's law, her going the same way as him? because here she is. Unusually tired, and a crow is a big bird, a crow is so strong, and it'll take one last push, yes, one last one and she thinks, get yourself up, stand up on your own two feet Lori Fitzgerald, and Lori

pushes against the stone wall at the bottom of the bridleway and she stands up, yes, here we go, she thinks, here we
are, and she feels the sky pressing down like a slab of stone,
like sandstone or slate and she thinks, so much stone, so
many stones and she looks down at her boots and she sees
the water weaving its way down into the valley and well,
all the things that mattered, she thinks, and she'll put the
coffee on, she'll feed the cat and she thinks, one last effort,
she thinks, Felix and Emile, beautiful little boys and she
pushes her boots over the loose stones.

Going up, yes, going on up, Lori thinks, and is that rain
now? rain again? because they hardly get a day without it at
this time of year and if she thinks of putting the bucket out
in the back room, well, no, she can't. No, she won't and she's
gone the same way as him now, unusually tired, she thinks,
yes, she's only a few steps behind him.

    The two of us, she thinks, yes, they've always been
a pair and really nothing's changed, no, they've got their
little house, they've got two cars out there on the lane,
a Commodore 64 under the chair in the porch.

    And she thinks, he never used that thing, he never
used the CD player either. Dead on arrival, he said, and she
pushes her boots over the loose stones and she thinks,
go on up, yes, once a pair, always a pair, that's the way it is,
she thinks, and it feels good to think like that, it feels like
warm air and she thinks, November, December, she thinks,
O come all ye faithful.

LORI STANDS BY THE GATE AND LOOKS DOWN THE
LANE, SHE LOOKS RIGHT THEN LEFT AND THERE ISN'T
ANYONE

Nobody around still, she thinks, and she pulls the gate
behind her and listens for the latch and now all she has to
do is get these legs of hers across the yard, and well, she's
passed more than a few hours out here in her time, God,
yes, this little yard of theirs and she looks over into the
next-door yard and she thinks, they're almost all holiday
cottages these days. You lose something, she thinks, yes,
something's lost, and she makes her way over to the front
door and she leans against it.

    And well, yes, quiet, she thinks, and she walks on in
through the porch and into the kitchen. Welcome home,
she thinks, and the November light is on its way out,
although it was only ever a small light, it was hardly a light
at all, she thinks, and she looks down at the flagstone floor
and she thinks, God of God, Light of Light and she sees the
coffee mugs sitting there on the side where she left them
this morning and well, if she's making herself a coffee she'll
have to get on and wash the mugs and she thinks, no need
to wash, plenty of clean mugs up there in the cupboard and
she looks over at the mugs sitting there on the side and
she thinks, the mugs won't clean themselves, no, they'll sit
there forever if she doesn't get on and wash them up and
she thinks, yes, she'll wash the mugs then deal with the
Chambéry and she thinks, boots off first Lori, because no,
she hasn't got the energy to go sweeping mud off the
kitchen floor right now and the sky is still pressing down,
she thinks, God, yes, the weight of the sky and she thinks,
forget the sky, and her hands are so cold, her hands are

almost frozen, but still, Lori thinks, the boots will have to come off and Lori puts her foot up on one of the kitchen chairs and if she can just grab hold of the end of a lace and tug. And she looks at her hands and she thinks, how can she tug? no, she can't do anything but swipe, one way and then the other way and she thinks, no, and well, the sky is pressing down on her chest, it's really falling in, she thinks, and she looks over at the window and she sees the sky sitting like a huge slab of stone and she thinks, go on, get on, and she rubs her hands up and down her thighs, she hits her hands against her thighs and she thinks her hands won't warm, and well, she'll just have to get on and wash the mugs anyway, yes, she may as well make herself useful, and Lori shuffles across the flagstones and she thinks, look at that mud now, yes, well, I've left a little trace after all, and it's quiet, yes, and the mugs are sitting there on the side where she left them this morning and she looks over at the clock on the wall, she looks out of the window and she sees that it's started spitting out there and well, she timed that well enough, didn't she? yes, out of the rain for once and she shuffles over to the kitchen table and well, look at that floor now, look at that mess, and she supposes she'll end up getting the broom out after all. The story of her life, she thinks, getting the broom for the kitchen floor, but come on, come on, get the *Chambéry* out of here, yes, come on you, she thinks, and there look, there on the handlebars is a little spider's web, yes, a lovely little web and she thinks, who's been spinning? who's been busy spinning over here? and she thinks, leave the *Chambéry*, leave it, because in all truth she hardly notices whether it's there or not these days and if a spider's built a home, she thinks, and she'll wash the coffee mugs instead. The *Chambéry* can wait, yes, the bike can stay where it is for a while because there really isn't any hurry with the bike and she shuffles back over to the sink and she thinks, mugs first, then she can get the place warmed up before she takes the weight off her feet and she looks at her hands and she thinks her hands are no good, her hands are no good at all, and she hears the rain against the window and she sees the coffee mugs sitting there side by side and she thinks, one for you and one for me, she thinks, tea for two and two for tea and Joseph should come down and help, she thinks, yes, come and help for once and she thinks, get up, get yourself up then, and she couldn't have changed anything. Fergus was already dead, yes, she'd thought he was a doll, and you only have to tip the body to get the eyelids to open and close, click-clack.

And of course it's quiet, although the cat, yes, where's the, and she thinks, don't pat, no, what good can patting ever, and she'll deal with the coffee mugs, she'll get the coffee mugs washed and put away because she couldn't get another coffee down her if she tried. Morning after morning with the coffee and now her hands have frozen solid, her hands are like blocks, all she can do is swipe, one way and then the other way.

And now the mugs have smashed, she thinks. Yes, our two mugs down there on the flagstones and she thinks, pick up the big pieces and then sweep, yes, she'll end up getting the broom out after all and well, she can, yes, she might as well, and Lori sits down on the kitchen floor. Get the big pieces up first, she thinks. First the big pieces. And her hands are frozen, her hands are solid and all she can do is swipe, one way, then the other way, that's all she's good for, she thinks, hardly good for anything. And she thinks, just wait for things to warm up, Lo, yes, just hold on down there for a while, although the November light has almost gone out, a little sound has come running.

( ) (   ) p   prototype

poetry / prose / interdisciplinary projects / anthologies

Creating new possibilities in the publishing of fiction and poetry
through a flexible, interdisciplinary approach and the production
of unique and beautiful books.

Prototype is an independent publisher working across genres
and disciplines, committed to discovering and sharing work that
exists outside the mainstream.
    Each publication is unique in its form and presentation, and
the aesthetic of each object is considered critical to its production.
    Prototype strives to increase audiences for experimental
writing, as the home for writers and artists whose work requires
a creative vision not offered by mainstream literary publishers.

In its current, evolving form, Prototype consists of 4 strands
of publications:
    (type 1 – poetry)
    (type 2 – prose)
    (type 3 – interdisciplinary projects)
    (type 4 – anthologies) including an annual anthology
    of new work, *PROTOTYPE*.

Lori & Joe by Amy Arnold
Published by Prototype in 2023

The right of Amy Arnold to be identified as author of this
work has been asserted in accordance with Section 77 of the
UK Copyright, Designs and Patents Act 1988.

Design by Matthew Stuart & Andrew Walsh-Lister
(Traven T. Croves)
Typeset in Marist by Seb McLauchlan
Printed in the UK by TJ Books

ISBN 978-1-913513-39-9

(type 2 – prose)
www.prototypepublishing.co.uk
@prototypepubs

prototype publishing
71 oriel road
london e9 5sg
uk

( )

ISBN 978-1-913513-39-9

9 781913 513399 >